Besos y besos para Graham

Abuelo y Abuela Shiel

Mayo 2001

Spanish Dictionary

Aladdin Books
Macmillan Publishing Company
New York

Maxwell Macmillan Canada
Toronto

Maxwell Macmillan International
New York   Oxford   Singapore   Sydney

Aladdin Books
Macmillan Publishing Company
866 Third Avenue
New York, NY 10022

Maxwell Macmillan Canada, Inc.
1200 Eglinton Avenue East
Suite 200
Don Mills, Ontario M3C 3N1

Macmillan Publishing Company is part of the Maxwell Communication Group of Companies.

Illustrations by Cathy Beylon/Evelyne Johnson Associates

First Aladdin Books edition 1992

Printed in the United States of America

10 9 8 7 6 5 4 3 2 1

Library of Congress Cataloging-in-Publication Data

Berlitz Jr. Spanish dictionary.—1st ed.
p.   cm.
Summary: Phrases and sentences illustrate the Spanish translation of more than 500 English words.
ISBN 0-689-71538-2
1. English language—Dictionaries—Spanish—Juvenile literature.
2. Spanish language—Dictionaries, Juvenile. [1. English language—Dictionaries—Spanish. 2. Spanish language materials—Bilingual.]
I. Berlitz Schools of Languages of America. II. Title: Berlitz junior Spanish dictionary.
PC4673.B39   1992   91-43927
423′.61—dc20

To the parent:

Learning a foreign language is one of the best ways to expand your child's horizons. It immediately exposes him or her to a foreign culture—especially important at a time when the world is more of a "global village" than ever before.

This *Berlitz Jr.* dictionary is the first Berlitz publication of its kind for children. The text has been approved by foreign-language experts and meets the Berlitz standard of quality. Teddy Berlitz and his friends bring Spanish to life by introducing simple words and phrases, without the need for grammatical drills or exercises.

The vocabulary has been chosen based on frequency lists, content of beginning language courses, and the natural interests of children. This controlled vocabulary makes it a perfect reference for beginning students and their parents. It is also an ideal companion to the *Berlitz Jr.* book-and-cassette kit.

Entries have been arranged alphabetically in English. Each word is followed by its Spanish counterpart and an English definition. An example sentence in both Spanish and English shows the word in context and is accompanied by a vivid illustration so children can associate pictures with meanings. Special illustrated "theme pages" reinforce the most basic vocabulary, such as numbers, colors, and common household words.

Every child has the ability to learn a foreign language, and *Berlitz Jr.* helps children to tap that potential. Enjoy sharing this dictionary—and watching your child's world grow.

Berlitz Publishing Company

AFRAID (TO BE): MIEDO (TENER)

The feeling you have when you are frightened or scared.

The small mouse is afraid of the big cat.
El ratón pequeño tiene miedo del gato grande.

AFTERNOON: TARDE

Afternoon is the part of the day between noon and nighttime.

Every afternoon, after he has lunch, Joey takes a nap.
Pepé duerme una siesta todas las tardes, después del almuerzo.

AIRPLANE: AVIÓN

Airplanes are big machines that can fly.

Jack flies everywhere in his small, red airplane.
Juanito vuela a todas partes en su pequeño avión rojo.

AIRPORT: AEROPUERTO

Airplanes land and take off at the airport.

Susana is leaving for vacation from the airport.
Susana se va de vacaciones desde el aeropuerto.

AMERICAN: AMERICANO

An American is a person who lives in the United States of America.

Teddy is proud to be an American.
Teddy está orgullosa de ser un americano.

AND: Y

And means also. We use the word *and* to join words and phrases.

Here are a proud, green rooster and a plump, brown hen.
Aquí están un gallo verde y orgulloso y una gallina marrón y redondita.

ANGRY: ENOJADO

You feel angry when you are unhappy and upset at someone or something.

Tim the Gorilla is very, very angry.
El gorila Timoteo está muy, muy enojado.

ANIMAL: ANIMAL

An animal is any living thing that is not a plant.

Dogs, bees, and frogs are all animals.
Los perros, las abejas y las ranas todos son animales.

2

ANSWER: CONTESTAR

When you answer someone, you reply to a question, call, or letter.

Teddy answers the teacher's question.
Teddy contesta a la pregunta de la profesora.

ANT: HORMIGA

Ants are small, fast insects that live in the ground.

Tina the Ant works very hard all summer long.
La hormiga Tina trabaja laboriosamente durante todo el verano.

APPLE: MANZANA

An apple is a crispy fruit that can be red, yellow, or green.

This apple is red and very shiny.
Esta manzana es roja y muy brillante.

APRIL: ABRIL

April is the fourth month of the year.

There are thirty days in April.
Hay treinta días en abril.

ARAB: ÁRABE

An Arab is a person born in Arabia.
Un árabe es una persona nacida en Arabia.

ARM: BRAZO

Your arm connects your shoulder to your wrist.

This gorilla has very, very long arms.
Este gorila tiene brazos muy, muy largos.

ASK: PREGUNTAR

Ask a question if you want to know the answer.

Joey is asking the policeman how to get to his friend Bill's house.

Pepé le pregunta al policia cómo llegar a casa de su amigo Guillermito.

ASTRONAUT: ASTRONAUTA

An astronaut is a person who travels to outer space.

This astronaut is exploring the moon.
Este astronauta está explorando la luna.

AUGUST: AGOSTO

August is the seventh month of the year.

In August it's very hot, and we eat lots of ice cream.
En agosto hace mucho calor y comemos muchos helados.

AUNT: TÍA

Your mother's or your father's sister is your aunt.
La hermana de tu madre o tu padre es tu tía.

BAD: MALO

Bad is the opposite of good. When people are being bad, they are doing something naughty.

This little monster is very, very bad.
Este pequeño monstruo es muy, muy malo.

BAG: BOLSA

A bag is a sack to carry things in.

Father Bear, Mother Bear, and Teddy are carrying bags of groceries.
Papá Oso, Mamá Oso y Teddy llevan sus compras en una bolsa.

BALL: PELOTA

A ball is a round object that is used in many kinds of games.

Teddy's favorite ball is red, white, and blue.
La pelota favorita de Teddy es roja, blanca y azul.

BANANA: PLÁTANO

A banana is a sweet, yellow fruit.

Gorillas really like bananas.
A los gorilas les encantan los plátanos.

BARBER: BARBERO

A barber cuts your hair when it's too long.

Barber Bob is cutting Father Bear's hair.
El barbero Tito le corta el pelo al Papá Oso.

BASKETBALL: BALONCESTO

Basketball is a fast game played with a ball and by two teams.

Jimmy the Giraffe is the tallest player on his basketball team.

La jirafa Jaimito es el jugador más alto del equipo de baloncesto.

BAT: BATE

A bat is a strong stick that is used to hit a baseball.

A famous baseball player autographed Teddy's bat.

Un famoso jugador de béisbol firmó el bate de Teddy.

BE: SER

To be means to exist.

Teddy is writing the verb TO BE on his paper.

Teddy está escribiendo el verbo SER en su papel.

BEACH: PLAYA

A beach is a sandy or rocky area by the ocean or a lake.

Teddy likes to build sandcastles at the beach in summer.

A Teddy le gusta construir castillos de arena en la playa en el verano.

BEAN: FRIJOL

A bean is a seed that we eat as a vegetable.

Lisa has left some red and green beans on her plate.

A Lisa le quedan unos frijoles rojos y verdes en su plato.

BEAR: OSO

A bear is a big animal covered with thick fur.

Polar bears are very white, and they love to play in the snow.

Los osos polares son muy blancos y les encanta jugar en la nieve.

BEAUTIFUL: HERMOSO

When something is beautiful, it is pretty to look at.

Rita the Rhinoceros thinks she is very beautiful.

La rinoceronte Rita cree que es muy hermosa.

BED: CAMA

A bed is a place to sleep when you're tired.

Teddy's bed is big and soft and has a warm, red blanket.

La cama de Teddy es grande y blanda y tiene una abrigada manta roja.

BEE: ABEJA

A bee is an insect that makes honey.

The bees fly around the flowers on Dora's hat.

Las abejas vuelan encima las flores del sombrero de Dora.

BEFORE: ANTES

Before means earlier in time.

Leo the Lion arrived at the theater before the movie began.

El león Leo llegó al cine antes de comenar la película.

BEHIND: DETRÁS

Behind means in back of.

The three little bears walk behind Mother Bear.

Los tres ositos caminan detrás de la Mamá Oso.

BELT: CINTURÓN

You wear a belt around your waist to hold up your pants or skirt.

This is Father Bear's favorite leather belt.

Este cinturón de cuero es el favorito de Papá Oso.

BICYCLE: BICICLETA

A bicycle has two wheels, handlebars, and pedals, and is fun to ride.

Teddy has just fallen off his new, red bicycle.

Teddy se acaba de caer de su nueva bicicleta roja.

BIG: GRANDE

Big is the opposite of small. It means large.

Joey is a very big elephant who went to the wedding of his small friend Gus.

Pepé es un elefante muy grande que fue al casamiento de su pequeño amigo, Gustavo.

BIRD: PÁJARO

A bird is an animal with wings, feathers, and a beak.

Chickens, penguins, and ducks are birds.

Los pollos, los pingüinos y los patos todos son pájaros.

BIRTHDAY: CUMPLEAÑOS

Your birthday is the day when you were born. You celebrate it every year.

Today is Teddy's birthday. He is six years old.

Hoy es el cumpleaños de Teddy. Cumple seis años.

BLACK: NEGRO

Black is a very dark color.

Maria spilled black ink on her paper.

María derramó tinta negra en su papel.

BLACKBOARD: PIZARRA

At school, you write on the blackboard with a piece of chalk.

Teddy is doing a sum on the blackboard.

Teddy hace una suma en la pizarra.

BLANKET: MANTA

A blanket is a cover that keeps you warm in bed.

It's cold today, so our friends cover themselves with a big, brown blanket.
Hace frío hoy, así que nuestros amigos se cubren con una manta grande y marrón.

BLOND: RUBIO

Blond hair is yellow or gold in color.

Dodo's hair is very, very blond.
El pelo de Dodo es muy, muy rubio.

BLUE: AZUL

Blue is the color of the sky when it's sunny.

Jane's eyes are as blue as the sky.
Los ojos de Juanita son tan azules como el cielo.

BOAT: BOTE

A boat is used to travel on water.

Cricket loves to row his little boat.
A Grillito le encanta remar en su pequeño bote.

BOOK: LIBRO

A book has pages with words and pictures on them for people to read.

Teddy's teacher is showing her class a very nice picture book.
La maestra de Teddy está enseñando un libro de dibujos muy bonito a la clase.

BOTTLE: BOTELLA

A bottle is used to hold liquids.

Joey is pouring a bottle of milk.
Pepé está echando leche de una botella.

BOX: CAJA

A box is a container used to hold things.

Matthew wants to put the candy in one of the boxes, but isn't sure which one.
Mateo quiere poner el caramelo en una de las cajas, pero no está seguro en cuál de ellas.

BOY: NIÑO

A boy is a child who will be a man one day.

All these boys are on the same baseball team.
Todos estos niños juegan en el mismo equipo de béisbol.

BRANCH: RAMA

A branch is the part of a tree that grows from the trunk and has leaves.

Our friend Sherlock is sawing off a branch, but I'm afraid he's going to fall along with it.
Nuestro amigo Sherlock está aserrando una rama, pero temo que se va a caer junto con ella.

BRAVE: VALIENTE

A brave person is someone who isn't afraid.

The ship's captain is very, very brave.
El capitán de esta nave es muy, muy valiente.

BREAD: PAN

Bread is a baked food that is usually made from flour, yeast, and milk.

With these two slices of bread, Teddy is going to make a sandwich.
Con estas dos rebanadas de pan, Teddy se prepara un bocadillo.

BREAKFAST: DESAYUNO

Breakfast is the first meal of the day.

Pete the Octopus always enjoys his breakfast.
El pulpo Pedrito siempre disfruta de su desayuno.

BRIDGE: PUENTE

A bridge is a roadway that is built across water.

Theo's small paper boat is sailing under the stone bridge.
El barquito de papel de Teo navega debajo del puente de piedra.

BROTHER: HERMANO

Your brother has the same mother and same father as you do.

Steven's big brother's name is Anthony.
El hermano mayor d'Esteban se llama Antonio.

BROWN: MARRÓN

Brown is the color of chocolate and toasted coffee beans.

This pony is brown, but his mane and tail are white.
Este caballito es marrón, pero su crin y su cola son blancas.

BUS: ÓMNIBUS

A bus is a large vehicle used to transport people.

This red double-decker bus is very crowded today.
Este ómnibus rojo de dos pisos está muy lleno hoy.

BUTTERFLY: MARIPOSA

A butterfly is an insect with four brightly colored wings.

This beautifully colored butterfly flies lightly everywhere.
Esta mariposa de hermosos colores vuela suavemente por todas partes.

BUTTON: BOTÓN

A button is a small object that is used to fasten clothes.

Here are three different buttons.
Aquí tenemos tres botones distintos.

BUY: COMPRAR

When you buy something, you pay money for it.

Mrs. Rabbit has gone to the market to buy some pears.
La señora Conejo ha ido al mercado a comprar unas peras.

CAKE: PASTEL

A cake is a sweet food that is baked in an oven.

Teddy has just eaten a large piece of his favorite cake.
Teddy se acaba de comer un gran trozo de su pastel favorito.

CALL: LLAMAR

When you want to talk to someone who is not near you, you call him.

Porcupine is using a pink phone to call his friend.
Puerco Espin está usando un teléfono rosado para llamar a su amigo.

CAMEL: CAMELLO

A camel is a four-legged animal that lives in the desert.

This friendly camel lives in the Sahara and can go days without drinking any water.

Este amigable camello vive en el desierto del Sahara y puede estar días sin beber agua.

CAMERA: CÁMERA DE FOTOGRAFIAR

A camera is used to take photographs or movies.

Teddy's father takes pictures with this new camera.

El papá de Teddy saca fotos con su nueva cámera de fotografiar.

CAP: GORRO

A cap is a small, soft hat.

These baseball players are wearing matching caps.

Estos jugadores de béisbol usan gorros iguales.

CAR: AUTOMÓVIL

A car is a four-wheeled vehicle with a motor that runs on gas.

Joey's small, green car has a flat tire.

El pequeño automóvil verde de Pepé tiene una llanta reventada.

CARPET: ALFOMBRA

A carpet is a large rug that covers the floor.

Freddy the Crocodile has just bought a magic carpet.

El cocodrilo Fredi acaba de comprar una alfombra mágica.

CARROT: ZANAHORIA

Carrots are crispy, orange vegetables that grow in the ground.

This must be the biggest carrot ever found.

Esta debe de ser la zanahoria más grande que existe.

CARTOONS: DIBUJOS ANIMADOS

A cartoon is a picture that makes you laugh.

In the afternoon, we sometimes watch cartoons on television.

A veces vemos dibujos animados en la televisión por la tarde.

CASTLE: CASTILLO

A castle is a large building where princes and princesses used to live.

Once upon a time, Merlin the Magician lived in this castle.

Érase una vez, en este castillo vivía el mago Merlin.

CAT: GATO

A cat is a small animal with soft fur and whiskers.

This cat is smiling because it's just seen a mouse.
Este gato sonríe porque acaba de ver un ratón.

CATERPILLAR: ORUGA

A caterpillar is an insect that looks like a hairy green worm. Caterpillars turn into butterflies or moths.

How many pairs of rollerskates does this caterpillar need?
¿Cuántos pares de patines necesita esta oruga?

CHAIR: SILLA

A chair is a piece of furniture that you sit on.

This chair is from Teddy's bedroom.
Esta silla es del dormitorio de Teddy.

CHEESE: QUESO

Cheese is a food made from milk.

Cheese is probably a mouse's favorite food.
El queso es seguramente la comida favorita de un ratón.

CHILD (CHILDREN): NIÑO(S)

A child is a young boy or girl.

Teddy and his good friends, Ann and Matt, are still children.
Teddy y sus buenos amigos, Ana y Mateo, aun son niños.

CHOCOLATE: CHOCOLATE

Chocolate is a food used to make candy. It's usually sweet and brown.

This chocolate bar is for Teddy and his friends.
Esta barra de chocolate es para Teddy y sus amigos.

CHRISTMAS: NAVIDAD

Christmas is a Christian holiday that is celebrated on December 25.

Teddy puts the star on the top of the Christmas tree.
Teddy coloca la estrella en la punta del árbol de Navidad.

CIRCLE: CÍRCULO

A circle is a perfectly round shape.

The full moon is a perfect circle.
La luna llena es un círculo perfecto.

CIRCUS: CIRCO

A circus is a traveling show with performing animals, clowns, and acrobats.

These clowns entertain the children at the circus.
Estos payasos divierten a los niños en el circo.

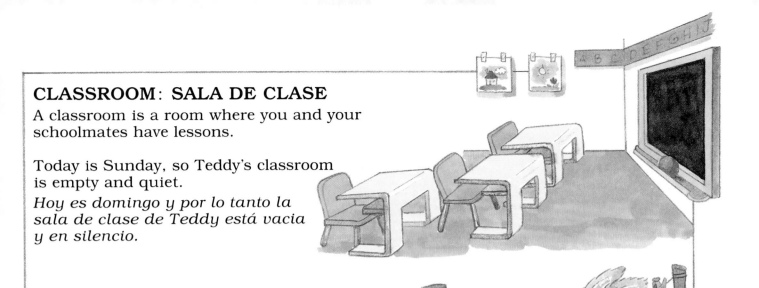

CLASSROOM: SALA DE CLASE

A classroom is a room where you and your schoolmates have lessons.

Today is Sunday, so Teddy's classroom is empty and quiet.

Hoy es domingo y por lo tanto la sala de clase de Teddy está vacia y en silencio.

CLEAN: LIMPIO

When something is clean, it does not have dirt on it.

Mrs. Rabbit is looking at her wash to see if it's really clean.

La señora Conejo está mirando si su ropa lavada está realmente limpia.

CLOCK: RELOJ

The numbers on the clock tell you what time it is.

It's midnight on the old tower clock.

Es medianoche en el viejo reloj de la torre.

CLOSED: CERRADO

When something is not open, it's closed.

The window in Teddy's bedroom is now closed.

La ventana del dormitorio de Teddy ahora está cerrada.

CLOSET: ROPERO

A closet is a small room used for storing things.

Teddy hangs up his jacket in the closet.
Teddy cuelga la chaqueta en el ropero.

CLOUD: NUBE

A cloud is a cluster of tiny water drops that floats in the sky.

Small, soft, white clouds float in the sky.
Las pequeñas nubes blancas y suaves flotan en el cielo.

COAT: ABRIGO

A coat is a piece of clothing that is worn outside in winter.

William is trying on a very nice blue coat, but it's too big for him.
Guillermo se está probando un abrigo azul muy bonito, pero es demasiado grande para él.

COFFEE: CAFÉ

Coffee is a hot drink for grown ups.

This cup of piping hot coffee is for Teddy's father.
Esta taza de café muy caliente es para el papá de Teddy.

COLD: FRIÓ

Cold is the opposite of hot. Ice cream, snow, and winter are all cold things.

Andy is cold because he forgot his coat.
Andrés tiene frío porque se le olvidó el abrigo.

COLORS: COLORES

If colors didn't exist, everything would be just black and white and gray.
Si no existieran los colores, todo sería negro, blanco, y gris.

COMB: PEINE

You use a comb to fix your hair.

Leo the Lion is fixing his beautiful mane with a big comb.
El león Leo se arregla su hermosa melena con un peine grande.

COMPUTER: COMPUTADORA

A computer is a special machine that we can use to play or to work with.

Teddy's parents bought him a new computer.
Los papás de Teddy le compraron una computadora nueva.

CONE: CONO

A cone is a shape with a circular base and a pointed top.

Un cono es un cuerpo de base circular que termina en punta.

COOK: COCINAR

Cook means to prepare food for eating.

Teddy and his father are cooking dinner.

Teddy y su papá están cocinando la cena.

COOKIE: GALLETA

Cookies are flat, sweet foods that taste good with a big glass of cold milk.

This big blue box is full of delicious cookies.

Esta grande caja azul está llena de galletas deliciosas.

COPY: COPIAR

When you copy something, you make it just like something else.

Joey shouldn't copy the answers from Andy's paper.

Pepé no deber copiar las respuestas del papel de Andrés.

COUNT: CONTAR

When you count, you say the numbers in order.

Amanda can count to ten on her fingers.

Amanda puede contar hasta diez con los dedos.

COUNTRY: PAÍS

A country is a land with its own government.

The United States, Mexico, and Japan are all countries.

Los Estados Unidos, México y Japón todos son países.

COWBOY: VAQUERO

A cowboy rides a horse and takes care of cattle on a ranch.

Teddy dressed up like a cowboy for Halloween.

Teddy se disfrazó de vaquero para la víspera de Todos los Santos.

CROCODILE: COCODRILO

A crocodile is a reptile with sharp teeth that lives in swamps.

Freddy is a friendly crocodile who lives in Florida where it's nice and warm.

Fredi es un cocodrilo amigable que vive en la Florida donde hace un calorcito muy agradable.

CROSS: CRUZAR

When you cross something, you go from one side of it to the other.

These three friends always cross the street carefully.

Estos tres amigos siempre cruzan la calle con cuidado.

CRY: LLORAR

You cry when you are sad and tears come out of your eyes.

Patty is crying because her doll is broken.

Patricia está llorando porque su muñeca se ha roto.

CUP: TAZA

You drink hot liquids from a cup.

Teddy uses this big, white cup to drink his hot chocolate in the morning.
Todas las mañanas Teddy usa esta grande taza blanca para tomar su chocolate caliente.

CUPBOARD: ARMARIO

A cupboard is a small cabinet used for storage.

The toys are in the cupboard.
Los jugetes están en el armario.

CUT: CORTAR

You cut things into pieces with a knife or scissors.

Teddy likes to cut shapes out of paper.
A Teddy le gusta cortar figuras de papel.

DADDY: PAPÁ

Young children call their father Daddy.

Teddy's daddy loves him very much.
El papá de Teddy lo quiere mucho.

DANCE: BAILAR

To dance is to move your body to music.

Cricket is always happy when he can dance.
Grillo siempre es feliz cuando puede bailar.

DANGER: PELIGRO

Danger means that something could harm or hurt you.

If you don't obey the danger sign, your car will fall off the cliff.
Si no obedeces el aviso de peligro, tu coche se caera por el barranco.

DAUGHTER: HIJA

A daughter is the female child of two parents.

Teddy's parents have one daughter.
Los padres de Teddy tienen una hija.

DAY: DÍA

There are 365 days in one year.

Today is a sunny day.
Hoy es un día soleado.

DECEMBER: DICIEMBRE

December is the twelfth and last month of the year.

Christmas is in December.
Navidad es en diciembre.

DEER: CIERVO

A deer is a forest animal with four legs and short fur. Male deer have antlers.

The deer live in the forest.
Los ciervos viven en el bosque.

DENTIST: DENTISTA

The dentist is a doctor who helps us keep our teeth healthy.

Hippo is really afraid of the dentist.
Hipo le tiene verdadero miedo al dentista.

DESK: ESCRITORIO

A desk is a table used for writing or reading.

The book is on the desk.
El libro está sobre el escrítorio.

DIFFERENT: DIFERENTE

When something is different, it is not like something else.

The blue sock is different from the red one.
El calcetín azul es diferente del rojo.

DINNER: CENA

Dinner is the last meal of the day.

Joey invited his friends Ladybug and Cricket to dinner.
Pepé invitó a cenar a sus amigos Mariquita y Grillo.

DINOSAUR: DINOSAURO

A dinosaur was an animal that lived millions of years ago.

Dino the Dinosaur is holding a red flower in his mouth.
El dinosauro Dino tiene una flor roja en su boca.

DIRTY: SUCIO

When something is dirty, it isn't clean.

Teddy is dirty because he played soccer.
Teddy está sucio porque jugó al fútbol.

DOCTOR: MÉDICO

A doctor is a person who helps sick people get well.

This doctor is running to visit a very sick patient.
Este médico corre a visitar un paciente muy enfermo.

DOG: PERRO

A dog is a four-legged animal that barks.

Bully the Dog looks tough, but he really isn't.
El perro Bul parece rudo pero en realidad no lo es.

DOLL: MUÑECA

A doll is a toy that looks like a person.

Annie is a very pretty rag doll.
Anita es una muñeca de trapo muy bonita.

DOLPHIN: DELFÍN

A dolphin is a sea mammal that is very friendly and playful.

Dan the Dolphin can jump through the rings.
El delfín Dan puede saltar a través de los anillos.

DONKEY: BURRO

A donkey is an animal that looks like a small horse.

David the Donkey refuses to carry baskets full of apples.
El burro David se niega a llevar cestas llenas de manzanas.

DOOR: PUERTA

A door is an entrance to a room or a building.

The milkman left two botties of milk in front of the door.
El lechero dejó dos botellas de leche delante de la puerta.

DOORBELL: TIMBRE

You ring the doorbell to let people know that you're outside.

Toby is ringing the doorbell.
Tobi toca el timbre.

DOWN: ABAJO

Down is the opposite of up.

Leo skis quickly down the slope.
Leo esquia cuesta abajo rápidamente.

DRAWING: DIBUJO

A drawing is a picture done with pencils, ink, or crayons.

Teddy is very proud of his drawing.
Teddy está muy orgulloso de su dibujo.

DRESS: VESTIRSE

To dress means to put on clothes.

Hippo dresses to go to school.
Hipo se viste para ir a la escuela.

DRINK: BEBER

To drink means to swallow a liquid.

Tom the Tiger likes to drink lemonade when it's hot.
Al tigre Tomás le gusta tomar limonadas cuando hace calor.

DRIVE: MANEJAR

To drive means to operate a car, bus, or truck.

Who's driving the fast red car?
¿Quien maneja el rápido coche rojo?

DRY: SECA

Dry means without water or moisture.

All the clean clothes are now dry.
Toda la ropa limpia ahora está seca.

DUCK: PATO

A duck is a bird that swims in water.

The small, yellow duck is learning to swim.
El pequeño pato amarillo está aprendiendo a nadar.

EAGLE: ÁGUILA

An eagle is a large bird with sharp claws and long wings.

The bald eagle is the symbol of the United States.
El águila es el símbolo de los Estados Unidos.

EAR: OREJA

An ear is the part of the body that is used to hear.

Rodney Rabbit has such long ears!
¡El conejo Roni tiene las orejas tan largas!

EARLY: TEMPRANO

Early means before the usual time. It is the opposite of late.

Mike woke up too early this morning.
Miguelito se despertó demasiado temprano esta mañana.

EASY CHAIR: SILLÓN

An easy chair is a comfortable piece of furniture to sit on.

Hippo's favorite easy chair is green.
El sillón favorito de Hipo es verde.

EAT: COMER

When you eat, you chew and swallow your food.

This mouse wants to eat the cheese, but the cheese is in the trap.
Este ratón quiere comerse el queso, pero el queso está en la trampa.

EGG: HUEVO

Baby chicks hatch from eggs.

This is a fresh, white egg.
Este es un huevo fresco y blanco.

EIGHT: OCHO

Eight is the number after seven and before nine.

Here are eight nuts in a row.
Aquí hay ocho nueces en fila.

ELEPHANT: ELEFANTE

An elephant is a huge animal that has big ears and a long nose called a trunk.

This friendly elephant works in a circus.
Este elefante amigable trabaja en un circo.

ENGLISH: INGLÉS

English is a language that is spoken in England, the United States, and Canada.

Do you speak English?
¿Hablas inglés?

ENVELOPE: SOBRE

Letters and cards are mailed in envelopes.

This envelope is for a birthday card.
Este sobre es para una felicitación de cumpleaños.

EVENING: ATARDECER

Evening is the time of day when it starts to get dark.

It's evening and our friends are watching the sun go down.
Nuestros amigos contemplan el sol al atardecer.

EXERCISE : EJERCICIO

An exercise is an activity that keeps our bodies healthy.

Mrs. Hippo does her exercises every morning.
La señora Hipo hace sus ejercicios físicos todas las mañanas.

EYE : OJO

An eye is the part of the body that is used to see.

Octopus and Kangaroo both have black eyes.
Pulpo y Canguro ambos tienen ojos morados.

FACE : CARA

Your face is the front part of your head.

Teddy's face is reflected in the mirror.
La cara de Teddy está reflejada en el espejo.

FAIRY : HADA

A fairy is a make-believe person with magical powers.

All fairies have special magic wands.
Todas las hadas tienen varitas mágicas especiales.

34

FAIRY TALE: CUENTO DE HADAS

A fairy tale is a story about magical people and their adventures.

"Goldilocks and the Three Bears" is my favorite fairy tale.
"Los tres osos y Bucles de Oro" es mi cuento de hadas favorito.

FALL: OTOÑO

Fall is the season before winter when the days get cool and the leaves fall off the trees.

In the fall the children must go back to school.
En el otoño los niños vuelvan a la escuela.

FAMILY: FAMILIA

A family includes parents, children, and lots of other relatives.

Teddy's family is not very big.
La familia de Teddy no es muy grande.

FARM: GRANJA

A farm is a place where animals are raised and crops are grown.

Julia grows corn on her farm.
Julia cultiva maíz en su granja.

FAST: DEPRISA

Fast is the opposite of slow. To be fast is to be quick.

I couldn't catch him. He was too fast!
No lo pude alcanzar. ¡Corría demasiado deprisa!

FATHER: PADRE

A father is a man who has one or more children.

Teddy's father has two sons and a daughter.
El padre de Teddy tiene dos hijos y una hija.

FEBRUARY: FEBRERO

February is the second month of the year.

In February it's cold and there's lots of snow.
En febrero hace frío y nieva mucho.

FINGER: DEDO

You have five fingers on each hand.

Theo hurt his finger with the hammer.
Teo se ha lastimado el dedo con el martillo.

FIRE: FUEGO

A fire is made when something is burning.

In winter there's always a fire in the fireplace.
En invierno siempre hay fuego en la chimenea del hogar.

FIREFIGHTER: BOMBERO

A firefighter is a person who puts out fires.

Bruno the Firefighter put out Mr. Crow's cigar.
El bombero Bruno apagó el puro del señor Cuervo.

FISH: PEZ

A fish is an animal with fins and scales that lives in the water.

This big fish loves to swim lazily.
A este pez grande le encanta nadar tranquilamente.

FISHERMAN: PESCADOR

A fisherman is a person who catches fish, for sport or as a job.

Teddy is a good and patient fisherman.
Teddy es un paciente y buen pescador.

FIVE: CINCO

Five is the number that comes after four and before six.

Here are five shiny red apples in a row.
Aquí hay cinco manzanas rojas y brillantes en fila.

FLAG: BANDERA

A flag is a piece of cloth with different colors and designs on it.

Tim is holding his club's flag.
Timoteo soporta la bandera de su club.

FLOWER: FLOR

A flower is the brightly colored part of a plant that has petals.

Teddy is watering his favorite flowers.
Teddy riega sus flores favoritas.

FLU: GRIPE

The flu is caused by a virus and makes you feel very sick.

Doggy didn't go to school today because he has the flu.
Perrito no fue a la escuela hoy porque tiene la gripe.

FLY : VOLAR

Fly means to move through the air with wings.

This bird is flying south for the winter.
Este pájaro vuela al sur para pasar el invierno.

FOG : NIEBLA

Fog is a thick cloud close to the ground.

There's so much fog that Mr. Hound can't see a thing.
Hay tanta niebla que el señor Sabueso no puede ver nada.

FOOT : PIE

The foot is the part of the body at the end of the leg.

Guess who broke his left foot while playing soccer.
Adivina quién se quebró el pie izquierdo mientras jugaba al fútbol.

FORGET : OLVIDAR(SE)

When you forget, you don't remember to do something.

Teddy forgot to buy orange juice.
A Teddy se le olvidó comprar jugo de naranja.

FOUR: CUATRO

Four is the number that comes after three, but before five.

Here are four juicy oranges all in a row.
Aquí hay cuatro naranjas jugosas todas en fila.

FOX: ZORRO

A fox is a bushy-tailed animal with beautiful reddish fur.

Frank is a very friendly fox.
Paco es un zorro muy amigable.

FRENCHMAN: FRANCÉS

A Frenchman is a native of France.
Un francés es un nativo de Francia.

FRIDAY: VIERNES

Friday is the fifth day of the week.

Every Friday, Rita takes dancing lessons.
Rita toma clases de baile los viernes.

FRIEND: AMIGO

A friend is someone you like and who likes you, too.

These two ladybugs are very good friends.
Estas dos mariquitas son muy buenas amigas.

FROG: RANA

A frog is an animal that has long hind legs, that croaks, and can live both in and out of the water.

Frogs love to go swimming.
A las ranas les encanta nadar.

FRUIT: FRUTA

A fruit is the part of a plant that holds the seeds. Apples, cherries, and oranges are all fruits.

Teddy's uncle, Pete, sells fruit at the market.
El tío de Teddy, Pedro, vende fruta en el mercado.

FULL: LLENA

When something is full, it's holding all it can.

This mug is full of soda.
Este jarro está lleno de soda.

FUNNEL: EMBUDO

A funnel is used to pass liquids from one bottle to another.

This funnel is used to fill bottles with oil.
Este embudo se usa para llenar las botellas con aceite.

GARAGE : GARAJE

A garage is a building where cars, buses or trucks are parked.

Many cars are kept in this garage.
Se guardan muchos coches en este garaje.

GATE : VERJA

A gate is an opening in a wall or fence.

Somebody had trouble jumping over the gate.
A alguien le costó trabajo saltar esta verja.

GERMAN : ALEMAN

A German is a native of Germany.
Un aleman es un nativo de Alemania.

GIRL : NIÑA

A girl is a female child.

Teddy's sister, Susan, is a girl.
Susana, la hermana de Teddy, es una niña.

GIVE : DAR

To give means to let someone have something to keep.

Penguin always gives his girlfriend flowers.
Pingüino siempre le da flores a su amiga.

GLASS : VASO

A glass is a container that is used for drinking.

These are delicate, elegant glasses.
Estós son unos vasos finos y elegantes.

GLOVE : GUANTE

A glove is a piece of clothing to wear on your hand.

Poor Pete the Octopus! He needs so many gloves!
¡Pobre pulpo Pedrito! ¡Necesita tantos guantes!

GLUE : COLA

We use glue to make things stick together.

Teddy spilled a bottle of glue.
Teddy derramó una botella de cola.

GOAT : CABRA

A goat is an animal with horns and a short pointed beard.

Goats like to bang against trees with their horns.
A las cabras les gustan golpearse contra los árboles con los cuernos.

GOLD : ORO

Gold is a yellow metal that is used to make jewels and coins.

This small gold ring belongs to Susan.
Este pequeño anillo de oro es de Susana.

GOOD: BUENO

When something is good, it pleases you. Good is the opposite of bad.

Froggy's ice cream is really good.
El helado de Ranita es muy bueno.

GOOD-BYE: ADIÓS

You say good-bye when you go away.

Teddy says good-bye to his friends.
Teddy les dice adiós a sus amigos.

GORILLA: GORILA

A gorilla is an animal from Africa with very long arms.

Gorillas love to swing from trees.
A los gorilas les gustan columpiarse en los árboles.

GRANDFATHER: ABUELO

Your grandfather is your father's father or your mother's father.

Teddy's grandfather reads him a fairy tale.
El abuelo de Teddy le lee un cuento de hadas.

GRANDMOTHER: ABUELA

Your grandmother is your father's mother or your mother's mother.

Teddy's grandmother is knitting him a sweater.
La abuela de Teddy le teje un suéter.

GRANDPARENTS: ABUELOS

Your grandparents are your father's parents or your mother's parents.

Teddy's grandparents live with him.
Los abuelos de Teddy viven con él.

GRAPES: UVAS

Grapes are small green or purple fruits that grow in clusters on a vine.

This is a beautiful cluster of grapes.
Este es un hermoso racimo de uvas.

GRASS: HIERBA

Grass is a green plant that grows in fields and lawns.

Ladybugs like to hide in the grass.
A las mariquitas les gustan esconderse en la hierba.

GRASSHOPPER: GRILLO

A grasshopper is an insect that has long hind legs and chirps.

Grasshoppers can hop long distances.
Los grillos puedan saltar largas distancias.

GREEN: VERDE

Green is the color of peas and of new grass in spring.

Maria is wearing her green skirt.
María tiene puesta una falda verde.

GUITAR: GUITARRA

A guitar is a musical instrument that is played by plucking the strings with the fingers.

Elvis played the guitar.
Elvis tocó la guitarra.

HAIR: PELO

Hair is what grows on your head.

Barber Bruce has just combed Leo's hair.
El barbero Bruce acaba de peinar el pelo de Leo.

HAMMER: MARTILLO

A hammer is a tool that is used to pound nails.

Mr. Rabbit is using a hammer to hang up some pictures.
El señor Conejo usa un martillo para colgar unos cuadros.

HAND: MANO

Your hand is the part of your arm below the wrist.

Can you count the fingers on this hand?
¿Puedes contar los dedos de esta mano?

HANDKERCHIEF: PAÑUELO

You use a handkerchief to blow your nose or wipe your face.

Mousie's handkerchief is big indeed.
El pañuelo de Ratoncín es realmente grande.

HAPPY: FELIZ

When you feel happy, you feel good inside.

Patty is happy when she can dance.
Patricia es feliz cuando puede bailar.

HAT: SOMBRERO

A hat keeps your head warm in winter and protects it from the sun in summer.

The gray hat is much too big for John.
El sombrero gris es demasiado grande para Juan.

HE: ÉL

He is a word for a boy or a man.

He is wearing a red T-shirt.
Él lleva una camiset a roja.

HEAD: CABEZA

Your head is the part of your body above the neck.

Teddy's teacher is holding her head.
La maestra de Teddy sostiene la cabeza.

HEAR: OIR

You hear sounds with your ears.

The elephant hears the sound of the drums.
El elefante oye el sonido de los tambores.

HEART: CORAZÓN

The heart is the part of your body that pumps blood. A heart is also a shape and the symbol of love.

Frank just drew a red heart.
Paco acaba de dibujar un corazón rojo.

HEAVY: PESADO

Something heavy weighs a lot and is hard to lift.

The suitcase is too heavy for Gus.
La maleta es demasiado pesada para Gustavo.

HELICOPTER: HELICÓPTERO

A helicopter is a machine that can fly straight up and down.

Captain Tiger rescues people with his red helicopter.

El capitán Tigre rescata personas con su helicóptero rojo.

HELMET: CASCO

A helmet is a hard hat that protects your head.

Penguin always wears his helmet when he plays football.

Pingüino siempre se pone su casco cuando juega al fútbol americano.

HELP: AYUDAR

When you help people, you do something for them.

Teddy is helping his friend put away the toys.

Teddy está ayudando a su amigo a guardar los juguetes.

HI: HOLA

Hi is what we say to our friends when we see them.

Teddy always says "Hi" to his uncle and to Joey.

Teddy siempre les dice "Hola" a su tío y a Pepé.

HIPPOPOTAMUS: HIPOPÓTAMO

A hippopotamus is a big African animal that spends a lot of time in rivers.

Hippos have gray skin.
Los hipopótamos tienen una piel gris.

HOLE: AGUJERO

A hole is an empty, hollow place in something.

Cats know that mice hide in holes in the wall.
Los gatos saben que los ratones se esconden en los agujeros de la pared.

HOME: HOGAR

Home is what we call the place where we live.

This nice little house is Teddy's home.
Esta linda casita es el hogar de Teddy.

HONEY: MIEL

Honey is a sweet, sticky food made by bees.

This jar is full of golden honey.
Este frasco está lleno de miel dorada.

HORSE: CABALLO

A horse is an animal with a long mane and tail. Horses are lots of fun to ride.

Bert is a small dappled-gray horse.
Berto es un pequeño caballo bayo.

HOT: CALIENTE

Hot means very, very warm. It's the way we feel in the summer.

It is hot in July.
Hace calor en julio.

HOTEL: HOTEL

A hotel is a building with many bedrooms where people stay when they are traveling.

Which city do you think this hotel is in?
¿En qué ciudad crees que está este hotel?

HOW MUCH: CUÁNTO

We ask "How much?" when we want to know the price of something.

Mrs. Rabbit wants to know how much she has to pay.
La señora Conejo quiere saber cuánto tiene que pagar.

Se venden zanahorias

HUNGRY (TO BE): TENER HAMBRE

You feel hungry when you haven't eaten in a long time.

Gus is very hungry and wants to eat the cheese.

Gustavo tiene mucho hambre y quiere comerse el queso.

I: YO

When you talk about yourself, you use the word *I*.

Cuando hablas de tí mismo, usas la palabra "yo".

ICE: HIELO

Ice is frozen water.

There's lots of ice at the North Pole.

Hay mucho hielo en el Polo Norte.

ICE CREAM: HELADO

Ice cream is a sweet food made from frozen cream and sugar.

Lou's favorite food is strawberry ice cream.

La comida favorita de Luis es el helado de fresa.

IMPORTANT: IMPORTANTE

When something is important, you should pay attention to it.

Vincent the Vulture always wants to seem very important.

El buitre Vicente siempre quiere parecer muy importante.

IN: EN

We use the word *in* to show that something is located inside or within something else.

Henry is in his cell.
Enrique está en su celda.

INDIAN: INDIO

An Indian is a native person of North or South America.

Teddy likes to dress up like a North American Indian.
A Teddy le gusta disfrazarse de indio norteamericano.

ISLAND: ISLA

An island is land that is completely surrounded by water.

The turtle is alone on a tropical island.
La tortuga está solo en una isla tropical.

ITALIAN: ITALIANO

An Italian is a person from Italy.
Un italiano es una persona de Italia.

JACKET: CHAQUETA

A jacket is a short coat.

This nice blue jacket belongs to Teddy's father.
Esta linda chaqueta azul es del padre de Teddy.

JAM: MERMELADA
Jam is a food made from fruit and sugar that you spread on toast.

Piglet ate all the blackberry jam.
Tocinillo se comió toda la mermelada de zarzamora.

JANUARY: ENERO
January is the first month of the year.

In January Andy likes to go ice skating.
A Andrés le gusta patinar sobre el hielo en enero.

JAPANESE: JAPONÉS
Japanese people come from Japan.
Los japoneses vienen de Japón.

JULY: JULIO
July is the seventh month of the year.

In July it's nice to go swimming.
En julio es agradable ir a nadar.

JUMP: SALTAR
When you jump, you spring into the air.

Cricket can jump very far.
Grillito puede saltar muy lejos.

JUNE: JUNIO
June is the sixth month of the year.

In June school is over for the summer.
Se acaba el año escolar en junio.

KANGAROO: CANGURO
A kangaroo is an Australian animal with powerful hind legs. Kangaroos carry their babies in pouches.

Kangaroos can jump very far and very fast.
Los canguros pueden saltar muy lejos y muy rápido.

KEY: LLAVE
You use a key to unlock doors.

This is the key to Teddy's room.
Esta es la llave del cuarto de Teddy.

KING: REY
A king is the ruler of a kingdom or country.

Leo the Lion is king of the jungle.
El león Leo es el rey de la selva.

KISS: BESO

A kiss is a touch with the lips to say *I love you.*

Baby Gorilla is happy when his mother gives him a kiss.
El bebé Gorila está contento cuando su mamá le da un beso.

KITCHEN: COCINA

The kitchen is a room where people cook meals.

Teddy gets a snack from the kitchen.
Teddy va a la cocina a buscar la merienda.

LADDER: ESCALERA

A ladder is a tool that you climb to reach high places.

The firefighter uses the ladder to reach the window.
El bombero usa la escalera para alcanzar la ventana.

LADYBUG: MARIQUITA

A ladybug is a very small beetle with bright red wings.

All ladybugs have black spots on their wings.
Todas las mariquitas tienen manchitas negras en las alas.

LAKE: LAGO

A lake is water that is surrounded by land.

The water in this lake is always clean and cool.
El agua de este lago siempre está limpia y fresca.

LAMP: LÁMPARA

You use a lamp to light your room when it gets dark.

This lamp is next to Teddy's bed.
Esta lámpara está al lado de la cama de Teddy.

LANGUAGE: IDIOMA

Language is the words we speak, read, and write. Different countries have different languages.

Teddy learns the Spanish language at school.
Teddy aprende el idioma español en la escuela.

LATE: TARDE

Late is the opposite of early.

Mr. Bear got to the station late and missed his train.
El señor Oso llegó tarde a la estación y perdió el tren.

LAUGH: REIR

To laugh means to make sounds when you think something is funny.

Tom the Tiger is laughing at a funny joke.
El tigre Tomás se ríe de un chiste gracioso.

LAWN: CÉSPED

A lawn is an area of grass around a house.

Piglet takes good care of his lawn.
Tocinillo cuida mucho su césped.

LAZY: FLOJO

A lazy person doesn't want to work or do anything.

The lazy cat is sleeping in the sunshine.
El gato flojo duerme al sol.

LEAF: HOJA

A leaf is part of a plant.

This leaf just fell off a tree.
Esta hoja se acaba de caer de un árbol.

LEAVE: PARTIR

To leave means to go away.

Mr. Elephant is leaving by airplane.
El señor Elefante parte por avión.

LEFT: IZQUIERDA

Left is the opposite of right.

The policeman signals with his left arm.
El policía señala con su brazo izquierdo.

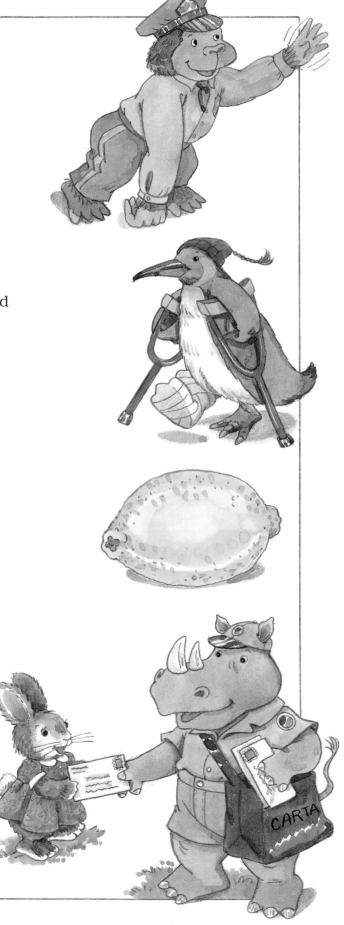

LEG: PIERNA

Your leg is the part of your body you stand and walk on.

Penguin went skiing and broke his right leg.
Pingüino fue a esquiar y se quebró la pierna derecha.

LEMON: LIMÓN

A lemon is a sour, yellow fruit.

This bright yellow lemon is now ripe.
Este brillante limón amarillo está maduro.

LETTER: CARTA

A letter is a message written on paper that you send to someone.

The mailman has a letter for Rachel.
El cartero tiene una carta para Raquel.

LIE : MENTIR

When you don't tell the truth, you lie.

When Pinocchio lied, his nose grew.
Cuando Pinocho mentía, su nariz crecía.

LIGHT : LUZ

Light is energy that lets us see things.

Porcupine was surprised by a sudden light.
Puerco Espin fue sorprendido por una luz repentina.

LIGHT : LIVIANA

Light is the opposite of heavy.

A feather is very, very light.
Una pluma es muy, muy liviana.

LIKE : GUSTAR

If you like something, it means it makes you happy.

This little mouse really likes cheese.
A este ratoncito le gusta mucho el queso.

LION : LEÓN
A lion is a huge cat that lives in Africa and Asia.

Leo the Lion looks ferocious.
El león Leo parece feroz.

LISTEN : ESCUCHAR
To listen means to try to hear carefully.

Tim the Gorilla listens to the radio.
El gorila Timoteo escucha la radio.

LIVE : VIVIR
To live means to be alive.

Teddy lives with his parents.
Teddy vive con sus padres.

LONG : LARGO
Long is the opposite of short.

Mrs. Hippopotamus's dress has a very long train.
El vestido de la señora Hipopótamo tiene una cola muy larga.

LOSE : PERDER
When you lose something, you mislay it and cannot find it.

Piglet is losing all the seeds in his sack.
Tocinillo está perdiendo todas las semillas de su saco.

LUNCH: ALMUERZO

Lunch is the second meal of the day.

Teddy takes his lunch to school in a paper bag.

Teddy lleva su almuerzo a la escuela en una bolsa de papel.

MAGICIAN: MAGO

A magician uses magic to do all kinds of tricks.

Teddy the Magician just made an ice cream cone appear.

El mago Teddy acaba de hacer aparecer un cono de helado.

MAILMAN: CARTERO

The mailman delivers letters and packages to your house.

Toby the Turtle is the fastest mailman in town.

La tortuga Tobi es el cartero más rápido de la ciudad.

MAN: HOMBRE

A man is an adult male person.

My dad is a very elegant man.

Mi papá es un hombre muy elegante.

MARCH: MARZO

March is the third month of the year.

March is always very windy.
En marzo siempre hace mucho viento.

MATCH: PARTIDO

A match is a game between two players or two teams.

Joey's team won the basketball match.
El equipo de Pepé ganó un partido de baloncesto.

MATH: MATEMÁTICAS

Math is the study of numbers, shapes, and measurements.

Teddy is not very good at math.
Teddy no hace muy bien las matemáticas

MAY: MAYO

May is the fifth month of the year.

Mother's Day is celebrated in May.
El Día de las Madres se celebra en mayo.

ME: ME, A MÍ, CONMIGO

Me is a word you use when you speak about yourself.

Anita wrote a letter to me.
Anita me escribió una carta.

MEAT: CARNE

Meat is the part of an animal we use as food.

A pork chop is one kind of meat.
Una chuleta de cerdo es un tipo de carne.

MEDICINE: MEDICINA

Medicine is what we take when we're ill to help us get well.

Oscar the Ostrich doesn't want to take his medicine.
El avestruz Oscar no quiere tomar su medicina.

MESS: DESORDEN

Something is a mess when things are not in the right place.

Look at the mess on this desk!
¡Mira qué desorden hay encima de este escritorio!

MIDNIGHT: MEDIANOCHE

Midnight is twelve o'clock at night.

The tower clock has just struck midnight.
El reloj de la torre acaba de tocar la medianoche.

MILK: LECHE

Milk is a white liquid that we drink. It usually comes from cows.

Someone left some milk in the glass.
Alguien dejó un poco de leche en el vaso.

MIRROR: ESPEJO

A mirror is a piece of polished glass that reflects your image.

Leo the Lion admires his new hairdo in the mirror.
El león Leo admira su nuevo peinado en el espejo.

MISS: SEÑORITA

We call an unmarried girl or young woman *miss*.

Miss Jackson is our teacher.
La señorita Jackson es nuestra maestra.

MOMMY: MAMÁ

Small children call their mother *Mommy*.

Teddy's mommy loves him very much.
La mamá de Teddy le quiere muchísimo.

MONDAY: LUNES

Monday is the very first day of the week.

Every Monday, Teddy goes swimming.
Teddy va a nadar los lunes.

MONEY: DINERO

Money is used to buy things.

Mr. Greedy is always counting
his money.
*El señor Avaro siempre está contando
su dinero.*

MONKEY: MONO

A monkey is a furry animal, with very long
arms and legs.

Monkeys love to eat bananas.
A los monos les encanta comer los plátanos.

MONTH: MES

There are twelve months in one year.

The calendar shows what month it is.
El calendario muestra qué mes es.

MOON: LUNA

The moon revolves around the earth in the
sky.

Wolfgang the Wolf howls at the moon.
El lobo Wolfgang aulla a la luna.

MORNING: MAÑANA

Morning is the part of the day before noon.

Mr. Leopard gets up early
in the morning.
*El señor Leopardo se levanta
temprano por la mañana.*

MOSQUITO: MOSQUITO

A mosquito is a small, flying insect.

Zip is the fastest mosquito I know.
Zip es el mosquito más veloz que conozco.

MOTHER: MADRE

A mother is a woman with one or more children.

Teddy loves his mother.
Teddy ama a su madre.

MOTORCYCLE: MOTOCICLETA

A motorcycle looks like a bicycle with a motor.

Teddy wears a helmet when he rides his motorcycle.
Teddy usa un casco cuando va en su motocicleta.

MOUNTAIN: MONTAÑA

A mountain is a high peak of land.

This high mountain has snow on top.
Esta montaña alta tiene nieve en la cima.

MOUSE: RATÓN

A mouse is a very small animal with a long tail.

The mouse ran up the clock.
El ratón subió al reloj.

MOUTH: BOCA

Your mouth is used to eat and speak.

Crocodiles have huge mouths.
Los cocodrilos tienen una boca enorme.

MOVIE: PELÍCULA

A movie is a film made of pictures that move.

Let's go see the movie!
¡Vámonos a ver la película!

MR.: SEÑOR

We call men *Mr.*

Mr. Rabbit reads the newspaper.
El señor Conejo lee el periódico.

MRS.: SEÑORA

We call a married woman *Mrs.*

Mrs. Bear is Teddy's mother.
La señora Oso es la madre de Teddy.

MUSIC: MÚSICA

Music is the sound made by the voice or by instruments.

This small band plays great music.
Esta pequeña banda toca música estupenda.

NAIL: CLAVO

A nail is a thin piece of metal with a pointed tip that is used to fasten things.

Pete hits the nail with the hammer.
Pedrito da al clavo con el martillo.

NAME: NOMBRE

A name is a word that you call something by.

Maria's name is printed on her shirt.
El nombre de María está estampado en su camisa.

NECK: CUELLO

Your neck connects your head to the rest of your body.

Giraffes have very long necks.
Las jirafas tienen un cuello muy largo.

NECKLACE: COLLAR

A necklace is a chain or a string of beads that is worn around the neck.

This necklace is made of beautiful green stones.
Este collar está hecho de unas hermosas piedras verdes.

NEEDLE: AGUJA

A needle is a slender piece of steel that is used to sew.

Here's a needle with blue thread.
Aquí hay una aguja con hilo azul.

NEW: NUEVO

Something new has never been used or worn before.

Julia is very proud of her new hat.
Julia está muy orgullosa de su nuevo sombrero.

NEWSPAPER: PERIÓDICO

You read the newspaper to find out what is going on in the world.

Mr. Rabbit can never read his newspaper in peace.
El señor Conejo nunca puede leer su periódico en paz.

NIGHT: NOCHE

Night is the part of the day when it is dark outside.

The moon and stars shine at night.
La luna y las estrellas brillan de noche.

NINE: NUEVE

Nine is the number after eight and before ten.

Here are nine red strawberries all in a row.
Aquí hay nueve fresas rojas todas en fila.

NO: NO

No is the opposite of *yes*.

The sign says that no hunting is allowed.
El aviso dice que no está permitido cazar.

NOISE: RUIDO

A noise is a sound, usually a loud one.

The band is making a lot of noise.
La banda está haciendo mucho ruido.

NOON: MEDIODÍA

Noon is twelve o'clock in the day.

It's exactly noon on the tower clock.
Es exactamente mediodía en el reloj de la torre.

NOSE: NARIZ

Your nose is in the center of your face.

Pinocchio's nose is now very long.
La nariz de Pinocho ahora es larguísima.

NOVEMBER: NOVIEMBRE

November is the eleventh month of the year.

In November all the leaves fall from the trees.
En noviembre, se caen las hojas de los árboles.

NURSE: ENFERMERA

A nurse is a person who looks after sick people.

Teddy's mother is a very good nurse.
La madre de Teddy es una enfermera muy buena.

OCTOBER: OCTUBRE

October is the tenth month of the year.

Halloween is celebrated on October 31.
Se celebra la víspera de Todos los Santos el 31 de octubre.

OFFICE: OFICINA

An office is a place where people work.

This is the office where Teddy's father works.
Esta es la oficina donde trabaja el padre de Teddy.

OLD: VIEJO

Old things have been used for a long time. Old people have lived many years.

This is a very old shoe.
Este es un zapato muy viejo.

ONE: UNO

One is a number more than zero and less than two.

Here is one big, green watermelon.
Aquí hay una sandía grande y verde.

ONE HUNDRED: CIEN

One hundred is ten times ten.

There are one hundred cherries in this basket.
En esta cesta hay cien cerezas.

ONE THOUSAND: MIL

One thousand is ten times one hundred.

Now there are one thousand cherries in this basket.
Ahora hay mil cerezas en esta cesta.

ONION: CEBOLLA

An onion is an edible bulb that has a very strong smell and taste.

Teddy's mother cries when she cuts onions.
La madre de Teddy llora cuando corta cebollas.

OPEN: ABRIR

To open is the opposite of to close or to shut.

The front door is open.
La puerta de entrada está abierta.

ORANGE: NARANJA

An orange is a juicy fruit with a thick rind.

We have to peel oranges before we eat them.
Hay que pelar las naranjas antes de comerlas.

OSTRICH: AVESTRUZ

An ostrich is a very large bird that lives in Africa.

Ostriches can't fly, but they can run very fast.
Los avestruces no pueden volar, pero sí pueden correr rápidamente.

OUT: FUERA

Out is the opposite of in.

Harry is now out of jail.
Quique ahora está fuera de la carcel.

PAGE: PÁGINA

A page is one side of a piece of paper in a book, magazine, or newspaper.

This page in Teddy's book has two big pictures.
Esta página del libro de Teddy tiene dos ilustraciones grandes.

PAINTER: PINTOR

A painter is a person who paints.

Teddy would like to be a famous painter.
A Teddy le gustaría ser un pintor famoso.

PAJAMAS: PIJAMAS

Pajamas are a shirt and pants that we wear when we go to bed.

Rhino and his wife are sharing a pair of pajamas.
Rino y su esposa comparten un par de pijamas.

PANDA: PANDA

A panda is an animal that lives in Asia and looks like a big black and white bear.

Pandas are a protected species.
Los pandas pertenecen a una especie protegida.

PANTS: PANTALONES

Pants are clothes with two long legs.

These pants are too big for Freddy.
Estos pantalones son muy grandes para Fredi.

PAPER: PAPEL

Paper is a material made from trees that you can write on.

The present is wrapped in pretty paper.
El regalo está envuelto en un bonito papel.

PARACHUTE: **PARACAÍDAS**

A parachute is used to drop people or things safely from an airplane.

Christopher's parachute opened right after he jumped out of his plane.
El paracaídas de Cristóbal se abrió después de que él saltó del avión.

PARENTS: **PADRES**

Your father and your mother are your parents.

Teddy's parents play with their children.
Los padres de Teddy juegan con sus hijos.

PARK: **PARQUE**

A park is a public garden with trees and grass and places where you can play.

This park has a slide, a see-saw, a sand box, and swings.
Este parque tiene una resbaladilla, un sube y baja, un cajón de arena y columpios.

PARROT: **LORO**

A parrot is a tropical bird with brightly colored feathers.

This parrot can speak.
Este loro sabe hablar.

PEA: **GUISANTE**

A pea is a small, round, green vegetable.

This pod has five peas in it.
Esta vaina tenía cinco guisantes.

PEACH: DURAZNO

A peach is a sweet, juicy fruit with a fuzzy peel.

This peach is now perfectly ripe.
Este durazno ahora está bien maduro.

PEAR: PERA

A pear is a green, sometimes yellow, fruit.

Pears are wider at the bottom than at the top.
Las peras son más anchas en la parte inferior que en la superior.

PEN: PLUMA

A pen is filled with ink and is used to write.

This is a special pen.
Esta pluma es una pluma especial.

PENCIL: LÁPIZ

You use a pencil to write or draw.

With this pencil we can color the sea or the sky.
Con este lápiz podemos colorar el mar o el cielo.

PENGUIN: PINGÜINO

A penguin is a short-legged bird that lives in Antarctica and can't fly.

Penguins look as if they're wearing tuxedos.
Los pingüinos parecen siempre vestidos de frac.

PHOTOGRAPH: FOTOGRAFÍA

We take a photograph with a camera.

Cricket is taking a photograph of seven ladybugs.
Grillo está sacando una fotografía a siete mariquitas.

PICTURE: CUADRO

A picture is a drawing or painting.

In this picture Piglet has a black eye.
En este cuadro Tocinillo tiene un ojo negro.

PIG: CERDO

A pig is a farm animal with a snout and a short, curly tail.

This pig is pink.
Este cerdo es de color rosa.

PINEAPPLE: PIÑA

A pineapple is a yellowish fruit that grows in the tropics and has a thick, rough peel.

This pineapple was grown in Hawaii.
Esta piña fue cultivada en Hawaii.

PINK: ROSA

Pink is a color made by mixing red with white.

Roses, flamingos, and baby pigs are pink.
Las rosas, los flamingos y los cerditos son de color rosa.

PLAY: JUGAR

To play means to do something for fun.

Teddy plays checkers with his friend.
Teddy juega a las damas con su amigo.

PLAY: TOCAR

To play means to perform music on an instrument.

Piglet is learning to play the trombone.
Tocinillo está aprendiendo a tocar el trombón.

PLEASE: POR FAVOR
Please is a word you say when you ask for something politely.

Please buy me an ice cream cone.
Cómprame un helado por favor.

POCKET: BOLSILLO
A pocket is a place that holds things.

Tim's pockets are empty.
Los bolsillos de Timoteo están vacios.

POINT: INDICAR
To point means to use your finger to show something.

Eddie is pointing with both his fingers and his toes.
Eduardo está indicando con los dedos de las manos y con los de los pies.

POLICEMAN: POLICÍA
A policeman helps keep public order and safety.

Pat is a very serious but very kind policeman.
Patricio es un policía muy serio pero muy amable.

POLITE: CORTÉS

When you are polite, you behave in a courteous and considerate manner.

Joey is always very polite and kind.
Pepé es siempre muy cortés y amable.

PORT: PUERTO

A port is a place where ships dock.

This is a very important and active port.
Este es un puerto muy importante y activo.

POTATO: PAPA

A potato is a vegetable that grows underground.

We eat baked potatoes for dinner.
Nosotros comemos papas asadas para cenar.

PRESENT: REGALO

A present is a gift you give on a special occasion.

Mrs. Rabbit bought many presents for Charlie.
La señora Conejo compró muchos regalos para Carlitos.

PRIZE : PREMIO

People get a prize when they win a contest or a competition.

Phil's team won first prize.
El equipo de Felipe ganó el primer premio.

PULL : JALAR

You pull when you want to move something toward you.

If they pull too hard, they'll tear the scarf.
Si jalan con demasiada fuerza, romperán la bufanda.

PUMPKIN : CALABAZA

A pumpkin is a big, orange fruit that grows on a vine.

Teddy made a jack-o'-lantern from a pumpkin.
Teddy escúlptó una cara en su calabaza.

PURPLE : MORADO

Purple is a color made by mixing red with blue.

Eggplants, plums, and violets are purple.
Las berenjenas, las cirueles y las violetas son moradas.

PUSH : EMPUJAR

Push is the opposite of pull. You push when you want to move something away from you.

Rhino is so clumsy that he pushes everybody.
Rino es tan torpe que empuja a todo el mundo.

QUEEN : REINA

A queen is the wife of a king or the head of a kingdom in her own right.

Queen Leona is the wife of King Leo.
La Reina Leona es la esposa del Rey Leo.

QUESTION : PREGUNTA

We ask a question when we don't know or aren't sure of something.

Teddy asks his teacher a question.
Teddy le hace una pregunta a la maestra.

RABBIT : CONEJO

A rabbit is a small, furry animal with a soft tail.

Rabbits have long, pointed ears.
Los conejos tienen las orejas largas y puntiagudas.

RADIO: RADIO

A radio is a machine that plays music and news broadcasts.

Tim has a small portable radio.
Timoteo tiene una pequeña radio portátil.

RAIN: LLUVIA

Rain is water that falls from the clouds.

When there's rain, we stay indoors.
Cuando llueve, nos quedamos en casa.

RAINBOW: ARCO IRIS

A rainbow is colors that appear in the sky after it rains.

There's a pot of gold at the end of the rainbow.
Hay una olla llena de oro al final del arco iris.

RAINCOAT: IMPERMEABLE

A raincoat is a coat you wear to keep dry in the rain.

Joey has a yellow raincoat.
Pepé tiene un impermeable amarillo.

READ: LEER

When you know how to read, you can understand written words.

Mr. Rabbit reads the newspaper every day.
El señor Conejo lee el periódico todos los días.

RED: ROJO

Red is the color of fire engines and ketchup.

Hearts and strawberries are red.
Los corazones y las fresas son de color rojo.

REFRIGERATOR: REFRIGERADOR

A refrigerator is a machine that keeps food cold.

This refrigerator is full of good things.
Este refrigerador está lleno de cosas buenas.

RESTAURANT: RESTAURANTE

A restaurant is a place to eat away from home.

This is a very famous and very good restaurant.
Este es un restaurante muy bueno y muy famoso.

RHINOCEROS: RINOCERONTE

A rhinoceros is a large African animal with one or two horns on its snout.

The rhinoceros has short legs, but it can run very fast.
El rinoceronte tiene las patas muy cortas pero puede correr muy rápido.

RICE: ARROZ

Rice is a white grain that is eaten for food.

Teddy eats rice with chopsticks.
Teddy come el arroz con palillos chinos.

RICH: RICO

Rich is the opposite of poor. Rich people have lots of money.

Mr. Greedy is very, very rich.
El señor Avaro es muy, muy rico.

RIGHT: DERECHA

Right is the opposite of left.

The policeman is signaling with his right arm.
El policía está señalando con su brazo derecho.

RING: ANILLO

A ring is a piece of jewelry that you wear on your finger.

This ring has a very pretty stone.
Este anillo tiene una piedra muy bonita.

RIVER: RÍO

A river is water that flows toward the sea or a lake.

Hippo is rowing down the river.
Hipo está remando río abajo.

ROAD: CARRETERA

A road is a wide path that cars travel on.

Do you know where this long road leads to?
¿Sabes a dónde llega este camino tan largo?

ROBOT: ROBOT

A robot is a machine that can do some things that people do.

This robot can stand on its head.
Este robot puede pararse de cabeza.

ROOF : TEJADO

A roof is the top part of a building.

This house has a red, slanted roof.
Esta casa tiene un tejado rojo e inclinado.

RUN : CORRER

Run means to move with your legs as fast as you can.

Teddy and his friends run in a race.
Teddy y sus amigos corren en una carrera.

SAIL : VELA

A sail is a large piece of cloth that catches the wind to make a boat move forward.

Jumbo's boat has a small sail.
El barco de Elefantón tiene una vela pequeña.

SALAD : ENSALADA

A salad is a cold food made with vegetables, fruits, or meat.

This is a lettuce and tomato salad.
Esta es una ensalada de lechuga y tomates.

SAND: ARENA

Sand is made of tiny pieces of rock.

In a desert there are tons and tons of sand.
En un desierto hay miles de toneladas de arena.

SANTA CLAUS: PAPÁ NOEL

Santa Claus brings children presents on Christmas Eve.

Santa Claus has a trumpet for Tim.
El Papá Noel trae una trompeta para Timoteo.

SATURDAY: SÁBADO

Saturday is the sixth day of the week.

Teddy and his sister watch cartoons on Saturday mornings.
Teddy y su hermana miran dibujos animados todos los sábados por la mañana.

SAUSAGE: SALCHICHA

A sausage is made of ground meat and spices.

Sausages are attached to one another with a string.
Las salchichas están atadas entre ellas con una cuerdecita.

SCALE: BALANZA
A scale is a machine used to weigh things.

Hippopotamus broke the scale.
Hipopótomo rompió la balanza.

SCHOOL: ESCUELA
School is a place where people learn things from teachers.

Children go to school every morning.
Los niños van a la escuela todas las mañanas.

SCISSORS: TIJERAS
Scissors are a tool used for cutting.

Teddy cuts paper with scissors.
Teddy corta papel con la tijera.

SEA: MAR
The sea is made of salt water.

Beaver takes his canoe to sea every summer.
Castor lleva su canoa al mar todos los veranos.

SEAL: FOCA

A seal is an animal that swims in the ocean and has smooth fur.

Sam the Seal is sleeping on a warm rock.
La foca Sami está durmiendo sobre una roca caliente.

SEASON: ESTACIÓN

Spring, summer, fall, and winter are the four seasons.

La primavera, el verano, el otoño y el invierno son las cuatro estaciones.

SEE: VER

To see means to look at something with your eyes.

Cats can see in the dark.
Los gatos pueden ver en la oscuridad.

SEPTEMBER: SEPTIEMBRE

September is the ninth month of the year.

In September, Teddy goes back to school.
En septiembre Teddy vuelve a la escuela.

SEVEN: SIETE

Seven is the number after six and before eight.

Here are seven purple plums all in a row.
Aquí hay siete ciruelas moradas todas en fila.

SHARK: TIBURÓN

A shark lives in the sea and has very sharp teeth.

Sharks are ferocious-looking animals.
Los tiburones son animales de aspecto feroz.

SHE: ELLA

She is a word for a girl or a woman.
Ella es la palabra para una niña o una mujer.

SHEEP: OVEJA

A sheep is an animal with curly hair that we use for wool.

Mrs. Sheep is knitting a sweater for her lamb.
La señora Oveja teje un suéter para su corderito.

SHERIFF: AGUACIL

A sheriff helped keep law and order in the Wild West.

Teddy's grandfather was a sheriff in Arizona.
El abuelo de Teddy fue un aguacil en Arizona.

SHIP: BUQUE

A ship is a big boat that can sail the seven seas.

A brave captain stays on board when his ship sinks.
Un capitán valiente se queda a bordo cuando se hunde su buque.

SHIRT: CAMISA

A shirt is a piece of clothing that covers the top part of your body.

Michael's white shirt isn't very white!
¡La camisa blanca de Miguel ya no está tan blanca!

SHOE: ZAPATO

Shoes protect our feet when we walk.

This is a comfortable running shoe.
Este es un cómodo zapato de correr.

SHOP: TIENDA

A shop is a place where you can buy things.

This shop has all kinds of toys.
Esta tienda tiene todo tipo de juguetes.

SHORT: CORTO

Short is the opposite of long.

Mrs. Hippopotamus's dress is much too short.
El vestido de la señora Hipopótamo es demasiado corto.

SHOWER: DUCHA

A shower is a spray of water to wash in.

Sammy's shower is a red watering can.
La ducha de Sami es una regadera roja.

SICK: ENFERMO

When you are sick, you do not feel well.

Doggy is sick, and so he stayed in bed.
Perrito está enfermo y por lo tanto se quedó en la cama.

SINGER: CANTANTE

A singer is a person who sings songs.

Annie is a great singer.
Anita es una cantante estupenda.

SISTER: HERMANA

Your sister is a girl who has the same father and mother you do.

Rachel is Theo's little sister.
Raquel es la hermana menor de Teo.

SIT DOWN: SENTARSE

To sit down means to rest your bottom on something.

Mr. Rabbit sits down in front of the television.
El señor Conejo se sienta delante de la televisión.

SIX: SEIS

Six is the number after five and before seven.

Here are six green pears all in a row.
Aquí hay seis peras verdes todas en fila.

SKI: ESQUIAR

Ski means to move over snow on skis.

Penguin loves to ski in the winter.
A Pingüino le gusta esquiar en el invierno.

SKIRT: FALDA

A skirt is a piece of clothing that women and girls wear.

This is Linda's favorite skirt.
Esta es la falda favorita de Linda.

SKY: CIELO

The sky is above you when you are outdoors.

There is a rainbow in the sky.
Hay un arco iris en el cielo.

SKYSCRAPER: RASCACIELOS

A skyscraper is a very tall building.

The Empire State Building is a famous skyscraper.
El Empire State Building es un famoso rascacielos.

SLEEP: DORMIR

To sleep is to rest with your eyes closed.

Piglet is sleeping under a tree.
Tocinillo está durmiendo debajo de un árbol.

SLEIGH: TRINEO

A sleigh is used to move about on snow or ice.

Santa Claus has a sleigh at the North Pole.
El Papá Noel tiene un trineo en el Polo Norte.

SLOW: LENTO

Slow is the opposite of fast.

Snails are very, very slow.
Los caracoles son muy, muy lentos.

SNAKE: CULEBRA

A snake is a long, thin reptile with no legs.

Snakes don't walk, they crawl.
Las culebras no caminan, se arrastran.

SNOW: NIEVE

Snow is rain that freezes.

Piglet and Theo are playing in the snow.
Tocinillo y Teo están jugando en la nieve.

SO LONG: HASTA LUEGO

So long is a friendly way of saying good-bye.

Teddy says, "So long," to his friend.
Teddy dice, "Hasta luego," a su amigo.

SOAP: JABÓN

Soap is used to wash and clean things.

This bar of soap is pink.
Esta barra de jabón es rosa.

SOCCER: FÚTBOL

Soccer is a game played with a round ball between two teams on a field.

Rhino plays soccer too roughly.
Rino juega muy bruscamente al fútbol.

SOCK: CALCETÍN

A sock is a soft cover for your foot.

Dino has only one red sock on.
Dino lleva puesto un solo calcetín rojo.

SOFA: SOFÁ

A sofa is a soft seat for two or more people.

Three people can sit on this comfortable sofa.
Tres personas pueden sentarse en este cómodo sofá.

SON: HIJO

A son is the male child of a mother and a father.

Teddy's parents have two sons.
Los padres de Teddy tienen dos hijos.

SORRY: PERDÓN, LO SIENTO

We say "Sorry" when we want to apologize.

Piglet says "Sorry" when he steps on someone's foot.

Tocinillo dice "Perdón, lo siento" cuando pisa a alguien en el pie.

SOUP: SOPA

Soup is a liquid that you eat with a spoon.

The tomato soup is very hot.
La sopa de tomate está muy caliente.

SPACESHIP: NAVE ESPACIAL

A spaceship carries astronauts to outer space.

This spaceship is traveling to Mars.
Esta nave espacial está viajando a Marte.

SPANIARD: ESPAÑOL

A Spaniard is a native of Spain.
Un español es un nativo de España.

SPIDER: ARAÑA

A spider is a small animal with eight legs.

Spiders weave very fine cobwebs.
Las arañas tejen telarañas muy finas.

SPINACH: ESPINACAS

Spinach is a vegetable with dark green leaves.

Mrs. Rabbit buys spinach for her children.
La señora Conejo compra espinacas para sus hijos.

SPORT: DEPORTE

A sport is a game that we play for fun and for exercise.

Pete the Octopus practices all kinds of sports.
El pulpo Pedrito practica todo tipo de deportes.

SPRING: PRIMAVERA

Spring is the season when the days get warm and the trees get new leaves.

In spring Ella plants beans in her garden.
En la primavera Ella siembra guisantes en su huerta.

SQUIRREL: ARDILLA

A squirrel is a small, furry animal that eats nuts.

Squirrels have long, bushy tails.
Las ardillas tienen la cola larga y espesa.

STAMP: SELLO

A stamp is a small piece of paper you put on a letter that has to be mailed.

This stamp is from Leo's Jungle Kingdom.
Este sello es del Reino de Leo, rey de la selva.

STAR: ESTRELLA

A star is a small, bright light in the night sky.

There are fifty stars on the American flag.
Hay cincuenta estrellas en la bandera americana.

STEAK: BISTEC

A steak is a piece of beef.

This is a broiled steak.
Este es un bistec asado.

STOP: DETENER

Stop is the opposite of go.

The policeman ordered Rhino to stop.
El policía ordenó a Rino que se detuviera.

STRAWBERRY: FRESA

A strawberry is a small, red, juicy fruit.

Strawberries are especially good with cream.
Las fresas son especialmente buenas con crema.

STRONG: FUERTE

If you are strong, you are physically powerful.

Elephants are very strong.
Los elefantes son muy fuertes.

STUDENT: ESTUDIANTE

A student is a person who goes to school.
Un estudiante es alguien que asiste a la escuela.

STUDY: ESTUDIAR

When you study, you try hard to learn.

Freddy studies hard for his exam.
Fredi estudía mucho para su exámen.

SUBMARINE: SUBMARINO

A submarine is a ship that travels under water.

This green submarine travels to the bottom of the sea.
Este submarino verde viaja al fondo del mar.

SUIT: TRAJE

A suit is made up of a jacket and a pair of pants or a skirt.

This suit has a blue jacket and gray pants.
Este traje tiene una chaqueta azul y unos pantalones grises.

SUITCASE: MALETA

We pack our clothes in a suitcase when we travel.

Teddy packed his suitcase yesterday.
Teddy hizo su maleta ayer.

SUMMER: VERANO

Summer is the hottest season of the year.

In summer, we gather the crops.
En el verano recogemos la cosecha.

SUN: SOL

The sun is a star that gives us light and heat.

On a clear day, the sun shines brightly.
En un día claro, el sol brilla fuertemente.

SUNDAY: DOMINGO

Sunday is the seventh day of the week.

Teddy's family goes to church on Sundays.
La familia de Teddy va a la iglesia los domingos.

SURPRISE: SORPRESA

A surprise is something unexpected.

Jane's present was a complete surprise.
El regalo de Juanita fue una sorpresa completa.

SWEATER: SUÉTER

A sweater is a warm piece of clothing that you wear on the top part of your body.

Andy and his friend are sharing a huge sweater.
Andrés y su amiga comparten un enorme suéter.

SWIM: NADAR

To swim means to move in the water.

Turtles, frogs, and fish love to swim.
A las tortugas, las ranas y los peces les gustan mucho nadar.

TABLE: MESA

A table is a piece of furniture with four legs and a flat top.

This table is big but not very high.
Esta mesa es grande pero no muy alta.

TAIL: COLA

A tail is the part of an animal's body at the end of its back.

Felix takes good care of his lovely tail.
Félix cuida mucho su hermosa cola.

TAKE: TOMAR

To take means to bring or to carry or to get hold of something.

The big cat takes a book from the shelf.
El gato grande toma un libro del estante.

TALL: ALTO

Tall is the opposite of short.

Giraffes are very tall animals.
Las jirafas son animales muy altos.

TAXI : TAXI

A taxi is a car that carries passengers for a fare.

This is a small, yellow taxi.
Este es un pequeño taxi amarillo.

TEACHER : MAESTRO

A teacher is a person who helps people learn.

Mrs. Bear is a very good teacher.
La señora Oso es una maestra muy buena.

TELEPHONE : TELÉFONO

We use a telephone when we want to talk to someone who is far away.

Who forgot to hang up the telephone?
¿A quien se le olvidó colgar el teléfono?

TELEVISION : TELEVISIÓN

A television shows pictures with sound in our homes.

There are lots of cartoons on television.
Hay muchos dibujos animados en la televisión.

TEN: DIEZ

Ten is the number after nine and before eleven.

Here are ten small, red cherries all in a row.
Aquí hay diez pequeñas cerezas rojas todas en fila.

TENNIS COURT: CANCHA DE TENIS

A tennis court is where you play tennis.

Tennis players have to be very fast on the tennis court.
Los tenistas tienen que ser muy rápidos en la cancha de tenis.

THANK YOU: GRACIAS

We say "Thank you" when someone does something for us.

Freddy the Crocodile says "Thank you" with a bow.
El cocodrilo Fredi da las gracias con una reverencia.

THEATER: TEATRO

A theater is a place where plays and concerts are performed.

Hippo sings opera in a small theater.
Hipo canta ópera en un teatro pequeño.

THIN: DELGADO
Thin is the opposite of fat or thick.

Sammy the Snake is very, very thin.
La culebra Sami es muy, muy delgado.

THINK: PENSAR
To think means to use your mind.

Teddy's father is thinking about his vacation.
El papá de Teddy está pensando en sus vacaciones.

THIRSTY: (TENER) SED
When you are thirsty, you want something to drink.

You can get very thirsty in the desert.
Podemos tener mucha sed en el desierto.

THREE: TRES
Three is the number after two and before four.

Here are three yellow bananas all in a row.
Aquí hay tres plátanos amarillos todos en fila.

THURSDAY: JUEVES
Thursday is the fourth day of the week.

On Thursday, Annie takes violin lessons.
Anita toma clases de violín los jueves.

TIE: CORBATA
A tie is a piece of men's clothing that is worn with a shirt and a jacket.

Teddy's tie is much too long.
La corbata de Teddy es demasiado larga.

TIGER: TIGRE
Tigers are big striped cats that live in Asia.

You can recognize a tiger by its black stripes.
Puedes reconocer a un tigre por sus rayas negras.

TIRED: CANSADO
When you are tired, you need to sleep or rest.

Andy is tired because he has walked all day.
Andrés está muy cansado porque ha caminado todo el día.

110

TOMATO: TOMATE

A tomato is a red fruit that we use in salads, sauces, and sandwiches.

Ripe tomatoes are bright red.
Los tomates maduros son de un rojo intenso.

TONGUE: LENGUA

Your tongue is part of your mouth, and it helps you to speak, to eat, and to taste your food.

Raymond wants to see his tongue.
Ramón quiere ver la lengua.

TOOTH: DIENTE

A tooth is one of the hard, white parts in your mouth.

Hippo has lost a tooth.
Hipo ha perdido un diente.

TOOTHPASTE: DENTÍFRICO

We use toothpaste to help clean our teeth.

Toothpaste comes in tubes.
El dentífrico viene en tubos.

TOWEL : TOALLA

A towel is a piece of cloth used to dry or wipe things.

Piglet is drying himself with a towel.
Tocinillo se está secando con una toalla.

TOWN : VILLA

A town is a small city.

Teddy goes to school in town.
Teddy va a la escuela en la villa.

TOY : JUGUETE

A toy is something children play with.

Dolls, blocks, and balls are all toys.
Las muñecas, los cubos y las pelotas son todos juguetes.

TRAFFIC LIGHT : SEMÁFORO

A traffic light tells cars and people when to go and when to stop.

Teddy stops because the traffic light is red.
Teddy se detiene porque el semáforo está en rojo.

TRAIN : TREN

A train moves on rails and carries people and things from one place to another.

James and his train ran through the fence.
Jamie y su tren atravesaron la cerca.

TRAVEL: VIAJAR

To travel is to go from one place to another.

Tim travels many miles in his small, red car.
Timoteo viaja muchas millas en su pequeño coche rojo.

TREASURE: TESORO

A treasure is something of great value.

Pirates are happy when they find a treasure.
Los piratas siempre están contentos cuando encuentran un tesoro.

TREE: ÁRBOL

A tree is a plant with a trunk, branches, and leaves or needles.

Firs and pines are trees that are always green, even in winter.
Los abetos y los pinos son árboles que siempre están verdes, aun en invierno.

TRUCK: CAMIÓN

A truck is a vehicle that carries big, heavy things.

Ralph drives a big, green truck.
Raúl conduce un camión grande y verde.

TRUMPET: TROMPETA

A trumpet is a wind instrument made of brass.

Cricket likes to hide in Rhino's trumpet.
A Grillito le gusta esconderse en la trompeta de Rino.

TUESDAY: MARTES

Tuesday is the second day of the week.

On Tuesday Annie studies English in class.
Anita tiene clase de inglés los martes.

TUMMY: BARRIGA

Your tummy is the part of your body between the chest and hips.

Hippo is proud of his tummy.
Hipo está orgulloso de su barriga.

TURKEY: PAVO

A turkey is a big bird that is raised for food.

We eat turkey for Thanksgiving.
Comemos pavo el Día de Acción de Gracias.

TURTLE: TORTUGA

A turtle is an animal with a hard shell.

Turtles are never in a hurry.
Las tortugas nunca tienen prisa.

TWINS: MELLIZOS

Twins are two children who are born at the same time to the same mother.

Some twins are identical.
Algunos mellizos son idénticos.

TWO: DOS

Two is the number after one and before three.

Here are two big, juicy pineapples.
Aquí hay dos piñas grandes y jugosas.

TYPEWRITER: MAQUINA DE ESCRIBIR

A typewriter is a machine with a keyboard that we use to write with.

This is Teddy's father's typewriter.
Esta es la máquina de escribir del papá de Teddy.

T-SHIRT: CAMISETA
A T-Shirt has short sleeves and no collar.

Andy's favorite T-Shirt is red.
La camiseta favorita de Andrés es roja.

UGLY: FEO
Ugly is the opposite of beautiful.

Bruno tries to make himself ugly.
Bruno pone una cara fea.

UMBRELLA: PARAGUAS
An umbrella is used to protect us from the rain.

Froggy closes his umbrella because it has stopped raining.
Ranita cierra su paraguas porque ha dejado de llover.

UNCLE: TÍO
An uncle is your father's or your mother's brother.
El hermano de tu papá o tu mamá es tu tío.

UNITED STATES: ESTADOS UNIDOS
The United States is a big country. The capital is Washington, D.C.

Los Estados Unidos es un país grande. La capital es Washington, D.C.

VACATION: VACACIONES

A vacation is a time when people do not work or go to school.

Hippo always spends his vacation in the water.
Hipo siempre pasa sus vacaciones en el agua.

VACUUM CLEANER: ASPIRADORA

A vacuum cleaner is used to clean floors and rugs.

Piglet has a very powerful vacuum cleaner.
Tocinillo tiene una aspiradora muy fuerte.

VEGETABLES: VERDURA

A vegetable is an edible plant.

Carrots, peas, and cauliflowers are all vegetables.
Las zanahorias, las arvejas y las coliflores todas son verduras.

VOLCANO: VOLCÁN

A volcano is a mountain that has been formed by molten rock.

An active volcano spits fire and lava.
Un volcán activo echa fuego y lava.

WAIT FOR: ESPERAR

To wait means to stay in a place until something happens or someone comes.

Cricket is waiting for his friend Piglet.
Grillito está esperando a su amigo Tocinillo.

WAKE UP: DESPERTARSE

To wake up is to stop sleeping.

Pat always wakes up when he hears a strange noise.
Patricio siempre se despierta cuando oye un ruido extraño.

WALK: CAMINAR

To walk is to go somewhere on foot.

Cricket walks to school.
Grillito camina a la escuela.

WALL: PARED

A wall is one side of a building or a room.

Pete the Octopus paints the wall blue.
El pulpo Pedrito pinta la pared azul.

WASH: LAVAR

To wash is to clean something that is dirty.
Lavar es limpiar algo sucio.

WATER: AGUA

Water is a liquid that falls to the ground as rain.

These two ladybugs are spilling water.
Estas dos mariquitas están derramando agua.

WEDNESDAY: MIÉRCOLES

Wednesday is the third day of the week.

Piglet goes to his gym every Wednesday.
Tocinillo va al gimnasio todos los miércoles.

WEEK: SEMANA

A week is made up of seven days.
Una semana se compone de siete días.

WET: MOJADO

Wet is the opposite of dry. Something wet has water or another liquid on it.

Leo the Lion has wet hair.
El león Leo tiene el pelo mojado.

WHALE: BALLENA

A whale is a large mammal that lives in the sea.

This whale lives in the Pacific Ocean.
Esta ballena vive en el océano Pacífico.

WHEEL : RUEDA

A wheel is a round piece of wood, metal, or rubber that can roll.

This wheel belongs to a cart.
Esta rueda pertenece a un carro.

WHERE : DÓNDE

We use *where* to ask a question about a place.

Where are Leo's glasses?
¿Dónde están las gafas de Leo?

WHICH : CUAL

We use *which* when we want to know which one.

Piglet doesn't know which cake to choose.
Tocinillo no sabe cual pastel escoger.

WHITE : BLANCO

White is the opposite of black. It is the lightest color.

Swans and polar bears are white.
Los cisnes y los osos polares son blancos.

WHO: QUIEN

We use *who* to ask which person.

Mrs. Mouse wants to know who is at the door.
La señora Ratón quiere saber quien está a la puerta.

WHY: POR QUÉ

We use *why* to ask the reason for something.

When we ask a question with *why*, we answer it with *because*.
Cuando hacemos una pregunta con por qué, la contestamos con porque.

WIND: VIENTO

The wind is the air that moves over the earth.

The wind is blowing across the wheat field.
El viento está soplando por el campo de trigo.

WINDOW: VENTANA

A window is an opening in a wall that lets in air and light.

The window is open.
La ventana está abierta.

WINTER: INVIERNO

Winter is the coldest season of the year.

In winter it's very cold, and it snows a lot.
En invierno hace mucho frío y nieva mucho.

121

WOLF: LOBO

A wolf is a wild animal that looks like a dog.

This wolf lives alone in the woods.
Este lobo vive solo por el bosque.

WOMAN: MUJER

A woman is a grown-up female person.

Mrs. Rabbit is a very busy woman.
La señora Conejo es una mujer muy ocupada.

WOODS: BOSQUE

The woods are an area with lots of trees.

There are many pine trees in the woods.
Hay muchos pinos en el bosque.

WOOL: LANA

Wool is a fiber made from the hair of a sheep.

Tim is knitting a sweater with red wool.
Timoteo está tejiendo un suéter con lana roja.

WORK: TRABAJAR

To work is to use energy to do a job.

Porcupine works hard all day.
Puerco Espín trabaja mucho todo el día.

WORLD: MUNDO

The world is where all people live.

Teddy's teacher shows her class a globe of the world.
La maestra de Teddy muestra un globo del mundo a la clase.

WRITE: ESCRIBIR

To write is to put words on paper.

Teddy is writing a letter to a friend.
Teddy está escribiendo una carta a un amigo.

YARD: JARDÍN

A yard is an area next to a house or building.

Teddy's mother is planting tulips in her yard.
La mamá de Teddy está plantando tulipanes en su jardín.

YEAR: AÑO

A year is a period of twelve months.
Un año es un periódo de doce meses.

YELLOW: AMARILLO

Yellow is a bright color.

Lemons and bananas are yellow.
Los limones y los plátanos son amarillos.

YES: SÍ

We say "Yes" when we agree with someone.

Teddy nods his head to say "Yes."
Teddy asienta con la cabeza, indicando "Sí."

YOU: TÚ, USTED

You refers to the person you are speaking to.
Tú se refiere a la persona a quien hablas.

YOUNG: JOVEN

Young means not old.

Piglet's sister is still very young.
La hermana de Tocinillo es muy joven.

ZEBRA: CEBRA

A zebra is an African animal.

Zebras look like small, striped horses.
Las cebras se parecen a pequeños caballos rayados.

ZERO: CERO

Zero is a number that means nothing.

Zero fruits all in a row.
Cero frutas todas en fila.

cero

uno

dos

tres

cuatro

cinco

seis

siete

ocho

nueve

diez

once

12 doce

13 trece

14 catorce

15 quince

16 dieciséis

17 diecisiete

18 dieciocho

19 diecinueve

20 veinte

21 veintiuno

22 veintidós

23 veintitrés

30 treinta

40 cuarenta

50 cincuenta

60 sesenta

70 setenta

80 ochenta

90 noventa

100 cien

La casa

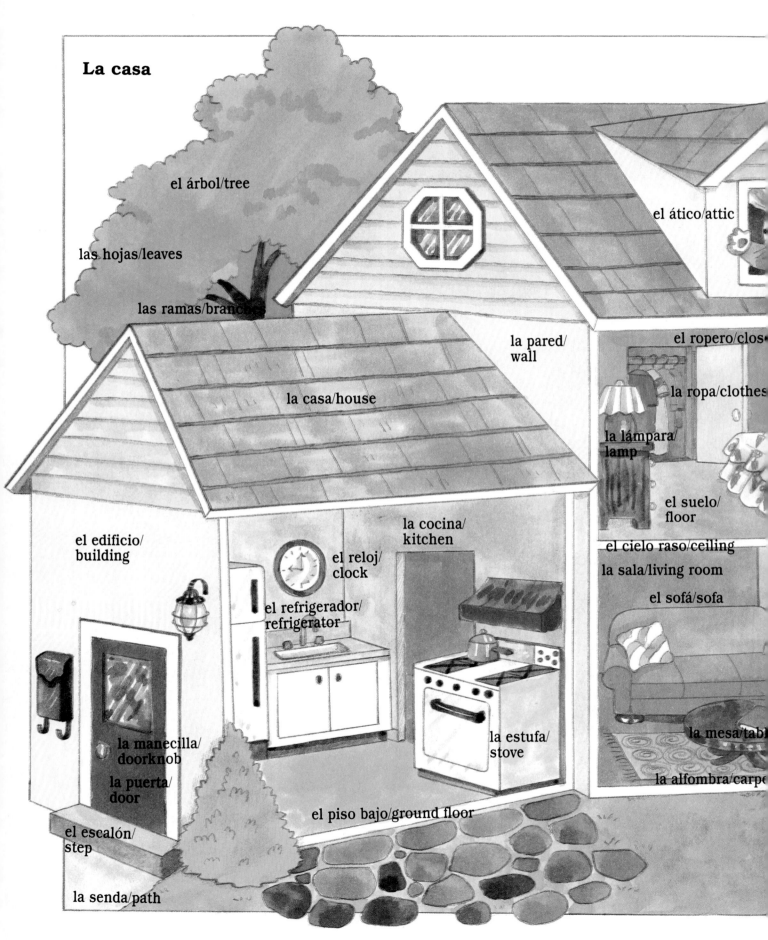

el árbol/tree

las hojas/leaves

las ramas/branches

el ático/attic

la pared/wall

la casa/house

el ropero/clos

la ropa/clothes

la lámpara/lamp

el suelo/floor

el cielo raso/ceiling

la sala/living room

el sofá/sofa

el edificio/building

el reloj/clock

la cocina/kitchen

el refrigerador/refrigerator

la estufa/stove

la mesa/tabl

la alfombra/carpe

la manecilla/doorknob

la puerta/door

el escalón/step

el piso bajo/ground floor

la senda/path

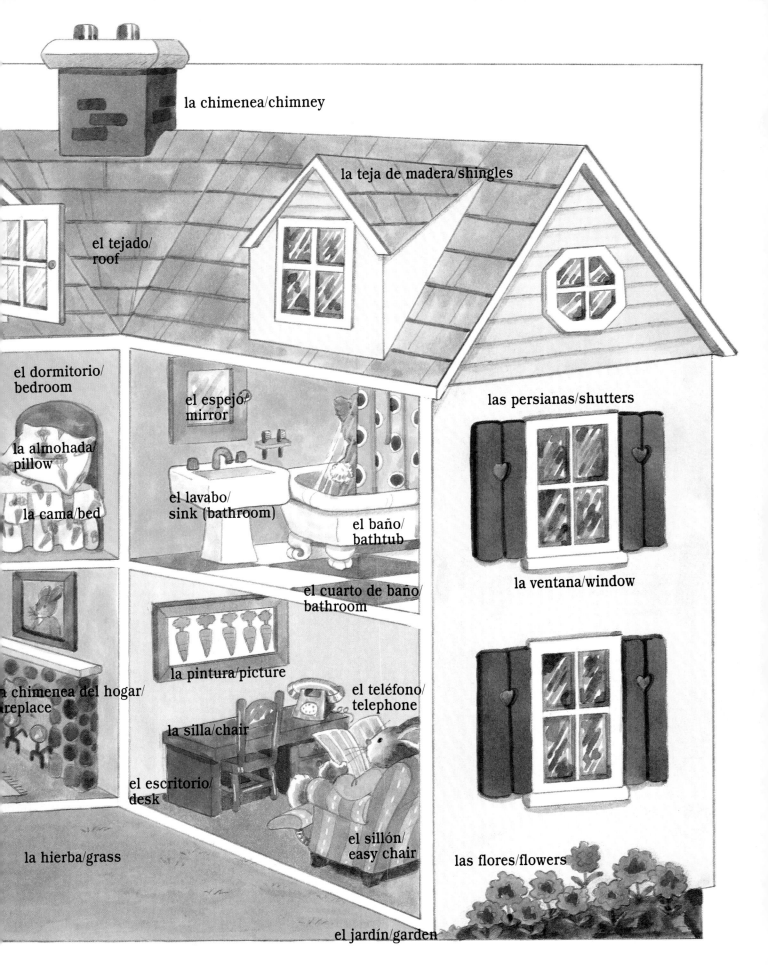

la chimenea/chimney

la teja de madera/shingles

el tejado/
roof

el dormitorio/
bedroom

el espejo/
mirror

las persianas/shutters

la almohada/
pillow

la cama/bed

el lavabo/
sink (bathroom)

el baño/
bathtub

la ventana/window

el cuarto de baño/
bathroom

la pintura/picture

a chimenea del hogar/
replace

el teléfono/
telephone

la silla/chair

el escritorio/
desk

el sillón/
easy chair

la hierba/grass

las flores/flowers

el jardín/garden

129

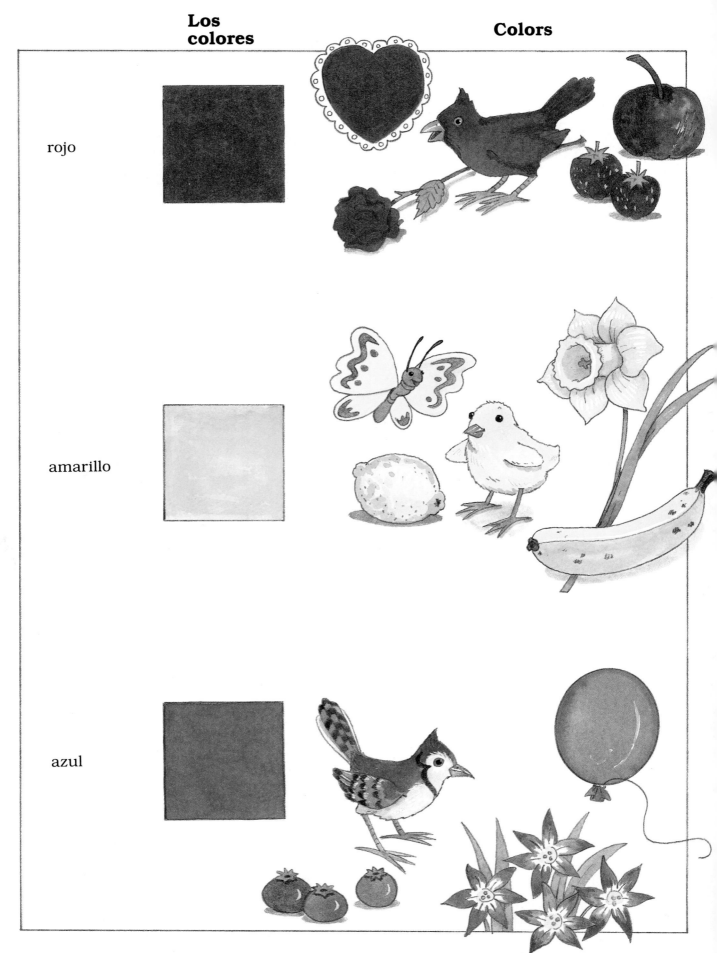

rojo

amarillo

azul

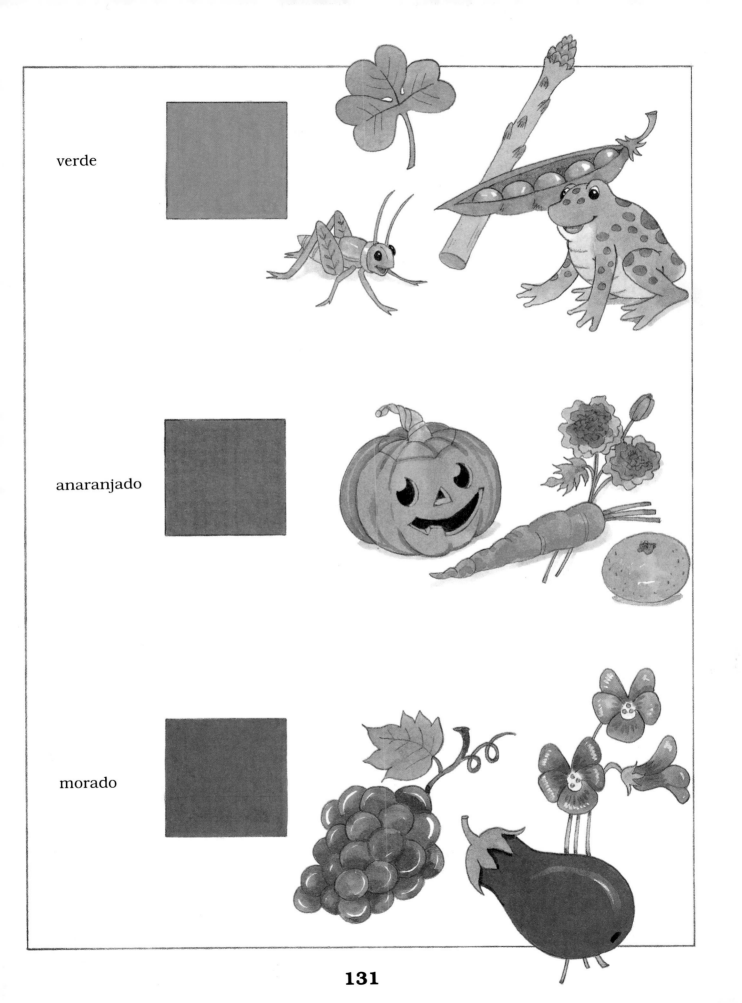

verde

anaranjado

morado

131

negro

marrón

blanco

rosado

americano

español

árabe

francés

japonesa

alemán

italiano

Las formas   Shapes

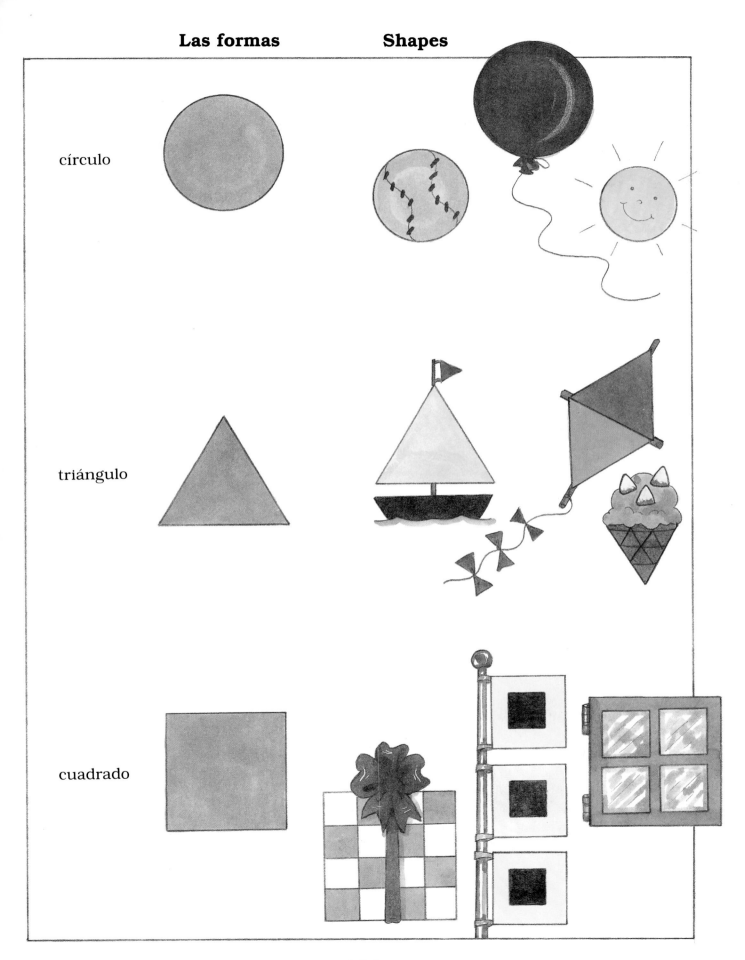

círculo

triángulo

cuadrado

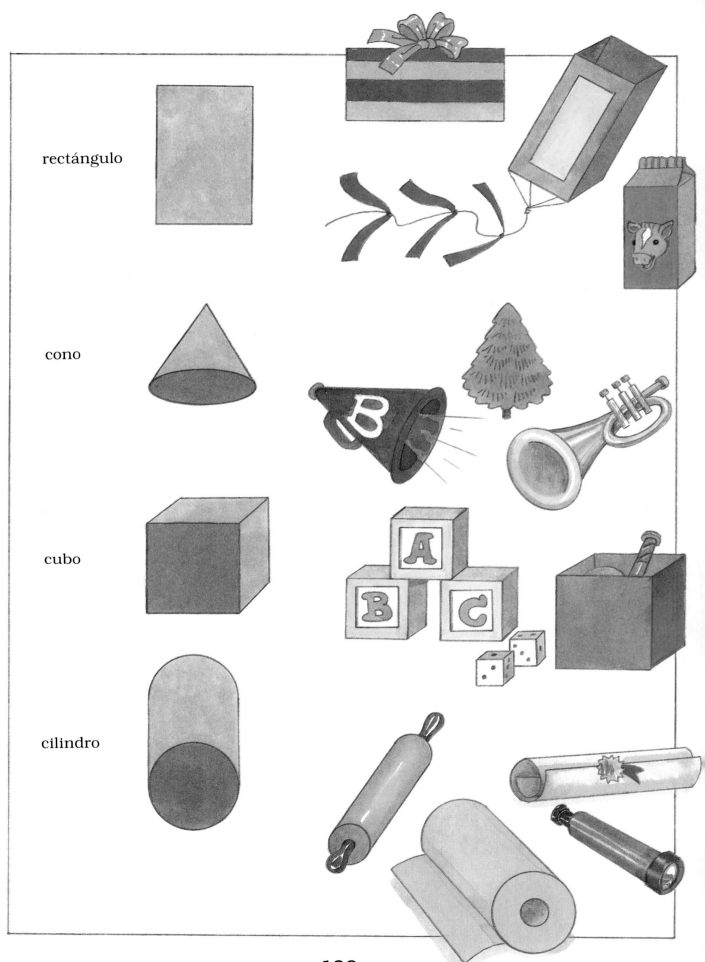

rectángulo

cono

cubo

cilindro

136

Los meses del año

The months of the year

enero

febrero

marzo

abril

mayo

junio

julio

agosto

septiembre

octubre

noviembre

diciembre

Los días de la semana   The days of the week

Monday
lunes

Tuesday
martes

Wednesday
miércoles

Thursday
jueves

Friday
viernes

Saturday
sábado

Sunday
domingo